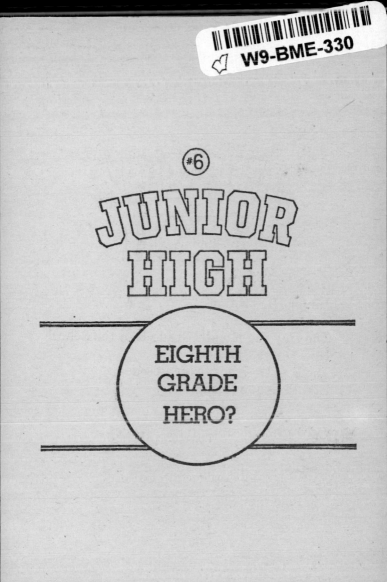

#6

JUNIOR HIGH

EIGHTH GRADE HERO?

JUNIOR HIGH

Junior High Jitters
Class Crush
The Day the Eighth Grade Ran the School
How Dumb Can You Get?
The Eighth Grade to the Rescue
Eighth Grade Hero?

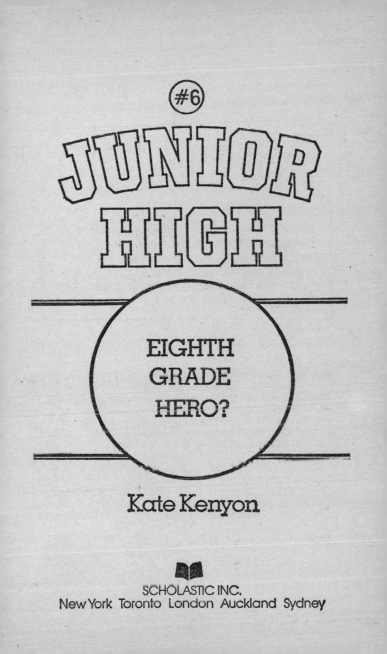

#6

JUNIOR HIGH

EIGHTH GRADE HERO?

Kate Kenyon

SCHOLASTIC INC.
New York Toronto London Auckland Sydney

For Ann Reit

ISBN 0-590-41054-7

12 11 10 9 8 7 6 5 4 3 2 1   7 8 9/8 0 1 2/9

Printed in the U.S.A.   01

First Scholastic printing, September 1987

Chapter 1

"If nine out of ten guys are cute," Susan Hillard said, "the tenth one goes to Cedar Groves Junior High School."

Nora Ryan looked across the lunch table to see how her best friend, Jennifer Mann, was taking Susan's remark. It was just what Nora thought. Jennifer's nose was scrunched up in disgust. Nora felt the same way.

"Oh, come on, Susan!" Jennifer said. "They may not all be gorgeous hunks, but they're not all awful, either."

Jennifer was tall, with shiny black hair and hazel eyes that usually sparkled, sometimes with fun, sometimes with compassion, and sometimes with anger. In spite of her apparent shyness, she was a fierce defender of people and animals in need, giving hours of her time each week to local charities and causes.

"Just like you to say that," Susan retorted. "You'll support any hopeless cause, no matter whether it's whales, old people, or the boys in our class."

Nora caught Jen's eye, the beginnings of a smile creeping around the edges of her mouth. She was hoping she could make Jen see the funny side of Susan's remark, but all she could make out in Jen's face was anger. When Susan made fun of Jen's causes, it made her volunteer work sound meaningless. And it wasn't. It meant a great deal to Jennifer.

Nora came to her aid. "Take this doctor's prescription, Jen, and ignore Susan. She's just crabby because of the lunch she ate. Anybody who thinks she can survive on three dill pickles and a diet soda for lunch is in trouble."

Nora had curly brown hair almost exactly matched by her brown eyes. She was always cool and assured, unflappable and logical. By fifth grade, Nora had made up her mind to be a doctor and had been working toward that goal ever since. It was hard for anybody to listen to Nora and not take her ambition seriously.

Jen laughed. It was just like Nora to try and blame somebody's mood on the food they'd eaten. "You are what you eat," was Nora's motto. So, today, that made Susan a pickle. Jen was glad that Nora was her friend — even if some of her ideas about food were a little odd.

"Go ahead and ignore me." Susan relented a little. "*That* may be easy. What's not easy is ignoring the specimens over there." She gestured across the pea-soup-green-walled room, where a group of eighth-grade boys were now pretending to be in a karate match. Susan turned away to show she really wasn't interested.

Jen and Nora looked at the boys. Mitch Pauley, the most athletic boy in the class, was squared off against Tommy Ryder. While Mitch was under the impression that he was born to be MVP, Tommy Ryder thought he was destined to be Don Juan. The girls thought they were both wrong.

Just then, Jason Anthony, everybody's candidate for Class Nerd, catapulted into the karate match from his skateboard. Somehow, in spite of the school's strict rule against skateboards, Jason managed to ride his constantly — even in the lunchroom. He stopped abruptly, leaped off the board, and threw his right leg high into the air with a powerful kick. If anybody had been in the way, they would have been in trouble. Next, Jason made two fast punches and a defensive move with his upper body. Then he ended the combination by pivoting on his left foot while hunkering into a crouch position, facing his enemy. His imaginary enemy. The boys applauded Jason. The slender boy with unruly red hair and freckles bowed to the applause.

"*Wow!*" Jen said. "It's a good thing Mitch and Tommy weren't in the way while Jason attacked."

"That was *something*," Nora agreed. He's *wonderful*."

"Give me a break," Susan said.

"I wonder if Jason has been studying karate," Tracy Douglas said, running her polished press-on nails through her permed blonde hair.

"Think he might be a black belt?" Nora asked.

"Well, maybe not black — " Jen said.

"Gray?" Tracy suggested. The girls laughed.

"No such thing as a gray belt, Tracy. But he *was* good," Nora said.

"Now don't get carried away," said Denise Hendrix, who, until then, had been sitting on the sidelines of the argument. Denise, whose father owned the successful Denise Cosmetics, had only recently come to the school. She'd lived all over the world and had gone to school in Switzerland before her father had decided it was time for his family to settle someplace where they could put down roots. Now Denise and her older brother, Tony, went to school in

Cedar Groves. It was a big change for them, but they were getting used to it — and Cedar Groves was getting used to them. Denise, a startlingly pretty blonde with picture-perfect features and soft blue eyes, had attracted a lot of attention in the school. In fact, she frequently still had a trail of boys behind her. It hadn't been easy for her to make friends — only admirers.

"How could we get carried away?" Nora asked.

"You already *have* gotten carried away," Susan said.

"Now wait a minute!" Jennifer said, warming up to her subject. "You didn't even see what Jason did over there. It was a near-professional karate move!"

"He was probably just falling off his skateboard," Susan said.

"I think he was great," Jen said.

"Personally, I think you're angry at Jason because he took some of the spaghetti off your plate yesterday. But that doesn't mean he's any worse then he ever was," Nora said to Susan.

"With his *hands*," Susan reminded her. She grimaced.

"That's how he always does it, Susan," Nora said. "At least that's how he stole my mashed potatoes last week."

"Yeah, Susan, that's just Jason," Jen cut in. "There's no reason to dislike him, or the other boys, any more today than you did yesterday."

Susan was getting uncomfortable. All of a sudden the girls were ganging up on her. She'd thought her remark about the boys was funny. She thought most of what she said was funny. And now they expected her to defend herself. Well, she wasn't going to give them the satisfaction. She stood up, stacking her books to leave the lunchroom.

"I have to go," she announced. "I can tell I'm not welcome at this meeting of the Jason Anthony fan club." She picked up the books and walked out as quickly as she could. She thought she could feel the heat of four pairs of eyes following her out of the lunchroom. She was wrong. The girls had more important things to talk about.

"Who's wearing what to Lucy's party on Friday?" Tracy asked.

Lucy Armanson was having a party for the whole class and just about everybody was going to go.

"Oh, groan," Denise said. "I never feel like I've dressed right for parties in Cedar Groves. I'm going to buy something for it, I just hope it will be right."

The three other girls stared at her in surprise. Denise was far and away the best-dressed girl in Cedar Groves. Not only did she have enough money to buy almost anything she wanted, but she had a real sense of how to put it all together so it looked terrific.

"You can buy anything in any store!" Tracy blurted out. "Of course it'll look right. You *always* look like a million dollars . . . which is probably what you have."

There was silence, and then everyone laughed at Tracy's simple outspokenness.

"What are you planning to buy, Denise?" Jen asked.

Denise shrugged. "Say, Jen, would you like to come to Dixon's with me and help me pick something out? *Please?*"

If Jen had heard right, there was a wistfulness in Denise's voice. Somehow it seemed very important to Denise that Jen come with her. The idea of helping Denise choose clothes made about as much sense to Jen as helping Albert Einstein with physics. But Jen readily agreed. Then, Denise looked at Nora. "Want to come, too?"

"No, thanks," she said. "I've got a biology project to work on. I'm going to be at my trusty microscope after school *and* early tomorrow morning."

Jen wondered about that. Nora's feelings always seemed a little bit hurt whenever Jen and Denise were doing something together. Nora liked Denise all right, but her liking never seemed to lead to their doing many things together. Jen thought Denise was really interesting. If Nora

7

didn't want to go with Denise, Jen felt it was Nora's loss.

Jen was so busy thinking about Nora that she didn't notice Jason on his skateboard, closing in from behind her. He really startled her when he reached over her shoulder and grabbed the maraschino cherry off the top of her fruit cup.

"Aaaarrrghhhhh!" she said, flinging her arms up over head.

"Nope, it's not Argh," he said. "It's just me, Jason." He popped the stolen fruit into his mouth and rolled out of the lunchroom.

"A black belt pain in the neck?" Nora suggested.

Jen laughed, but there was another image coming to her. She saw Jason's cool karate moves from earlier. Before she knew it, Jen had a picture of Jason in a white karate *gi*, black belt around his waist, registering his hands and feet with the police as deadly weapons. There was something wrong with the picture, but she wasn't sure what it was.

Chapter 2

Susan shifted her books and papers from her right arm to her left as she stormed down the hall. She couldn't believe how stubborn Jennifer had been about Jason Anthony.

Her anger grew. She walked faster, heading for the girls' room. She was a little afraid she might start crying before she got there. Two papers flew off the top of the stack she carried. She turned around and leaned over to pick them up. But as she reached for them, everything she was carrying slipped out of her grasp and her looseleaf notebook sprang open, spewing papers across the nearly deserted hall.

She began pulling her papers and books toward her. Then, she heard footsteps. Susan glanced up. Steve Crowley was coming her way.

Susan thought Steve was one of the few normal boys in the class — maybe even cute, with his dark brown hair, blue eyes, and his friendly smile. If she were going to go out with one of the boys in the class, it would probably be Steve, she decided.

Steve looked down the hall in front of him and saw Susan picking up scattered books and papers.

"I'll be right there," he called. "Susan? Is that you?" He squinted in the dim light.

"Yeah, it's me surrounded by this mess," she said coyly.

"I'll help you surround the mess," Steve offered, picking up some papers on his way.

Susan liked the way Steve was always nice to everybody — as if he didn't dislike anybody. In some people, that could be a really phony act, but in Steve, it was genuine.

Steve picked up Susan's American History book and handed it to her. "Here's another one," he said, reaching for a copy of *Jane Eyre*. "How'd it get so far away from the others?" he asked.

"I threw it," Susan admitted.

Steve look surprised. "You must have been very upset."

"I was, actually," Susan said. "I was upset about Jen and Nora. The two of them seem to be falling for Jason Anthony!"

Susan knew that wasn't what had just happened in the lunchroom, but maybe it wouldn't hurt her if Steve *thought* that was what had happened. She piled the last book on the stack and talked to Steve while she reorganized her looseleaf. Susan told him her version of what had gone on at the girls' table.

"So after Jason did whatever he did, Jen and Nora kept telling everybody how *wonderful* he was and even said they thought he was a black belt! Can you believe it?"

Steve stared at Susan, trying to understand what she was telling him. It was so unlike her to go out of her way to say something nice about anybody, but she seemed to be telling him how Nora and Jen had stood up for Jason when he'd really needed somebody on his side. Steve smiled, thinking about his friends. It really was like them to see the good side of somebody like Jason. Susan would have a hard time seeing the good side of anybody. Jen and Nora are the *wonderful* ones, Steve thought.

"I don't mean to be talking about people behind their backs or anything, but I thought you ought to know what's going on," Susan said.

"Thanks, Susan," said Steve thoughtfully. "I'll see you around" he said, and wandered off.

She hoped so.

Jennifer and Denise hopped off the bus

at the Twin Rivers Mall ready to take the stores by storm.

Jen hadn't decided if anything serious was on Denise's mind. They had spent the entire bus ride figuring out which stores they'd go to. They'd narrowed the options down to about eight. And they'd agreed that their first stop would definitely be Dixon's.

"Oh, look!" Jen said. "There's a sale on nail polish at Bradley's." They went to Bradley's first.

While they looked at colors, Denise suddenly turned to Jen. "You know, Jen, I really admire all the good things you do for people. Like the work for Save the Whales and the Cedar Groves Nursing Home."

"Would you like to work at the nursing home with me?" Jen asked. She was always looking for volunteers.

"No," Denise said wistfully, "but I wish there was *something* I could do to make people forget how rich they think I am. It seems like it's the only thing a lot of people know about me, and even when they know more about me it's sometimes the only thing they remember."

Jen looked at Denise and understood why Denise had particularly wanted to be with a friend today. She could see the hurt in Denise's face. "Is this because of what Tracy said at lunch today?"

"Yes and no." Denise fiddled with nail polish bottles on the rack, thinking about her answer. It was hard to explain. "It wasn't *just* Tracy. It's really almost everybody, except you. It was just Tracy *today*. Jen, when people think of you, they think of somebody who is always doing good things for others. They think of you as someone who *cares*. *That's* the way I'd like people to think of me."

Jen was astonished. She couldn't imagine Denise Hendrix being envious of her — or of anybody else. Denise suddenly looked uncomfortable, as if she was sorry she'd spoken so openly.

"Hey, look at this!" Jen said, quickly changing the subject. Her eyes lighted on a terrific bargain. "Here's a sampler of five nail polishes — all different colors — for one dollar."

"Are the colors nice or horrible?" Denise asked with relief.

"Nice," Jen said. Then she looked again. "Mostly. Anyway, it's too good a bargain. I have to buy it." She picked up the sampler.

They made their way to the checkout counter, picking up other things on the way: orange sticks, cuticle oil, emery boards, nail polish remover, and a clear gloss.

"The nail polish was a dollar, and the rest of the stuff was over six dollars. I'm not sure it was such a bargain," Jen said, laughing on her way out of Bradley's.

"We'll find bargains at Dixon's!" Denise said reassuringly.

As they left Bradley's, Steve Crowley emerged from behind the candy section where he'd been hiding. The next day was his mother's birthday, and he was hoping to find a gift for her. There hadn't been anything he wanted at Bradley's, and he'd been about to ask Jen and Denise to help him, but then they'd started having such a serious conversation that he didn't want to interrupt it. So he'd hidden — and listened.

Denise, of course, was absolutely right about Jen, Steve thought. She was the kindest, most generous and caring person he knew. If anybody needed help, Jen was there. She was very serious about her work with Save the Whales, and the people in the nursing home waited for her every Saturday afternoon.

He stepped out of Bradley's and began walking through the mall, totally uninspired about a present for his mother. The bookstore window was full of travel books about Japan. Swell. The shoe store was featuring orthopedic shoes. Not right for a birthday. He was searching the window of the housewares store when he saw Jen and Denise again. They didn't see him.

Nearby, a little boy was giving away

kittens. Jen and Denise stopped to play with them for a moment. Steve watched Jen. Suddenly, the basket tipped and the six kittens spilled out and scrambled away — or at least they tried to. While Denise watched in confusion and the little boy cried, Jen gently scooped up the kittens two at a time, brought them back, and re-deposited them in the basket. Then, she gave the little boy a tissue and comforted him.

For Steve, the moment froze. At that second, he saw Jen as he'd never seen her before. She was kind, loving and, most of all, beautiful — something he'd never actually noticed before. He'd known her all his life, but now he realized that he'd never *really* known her. A wave broke under his heart. He was in love.

He wanted to go over to her and speak, but when he tried his voice, it wouldn't work, and he was afraid he'd just say something stupid. He gulped, as if he were swallowing his new discovery, and walked away quickly.

He decided to buy his mother a box of imported chocolates and go home. To think about Jennifer Mann. Jen, Jenny, Jennifer Mann.

At Dixon's Junior Shop, Jen and Denise browsed through the racks, looking for a top to go with Denise's blue-and-white-striped straight skirt.

"I never can decide whether I love shopping, or I hate shopping," Jen confessed to Denise.

Denise shook her head in wonder. "Love it," she said. "I love it."

"That's because you're so good at it," Jen told her.

"Look, here's a bright print that might work — if I could find a T-shirt to go under it. Or how about this plaid? It's kind of offbeat," Denise said.

"Plaids and stripes?" Jen asked.

"Very 'in,'" Denise assured her. She knew that if Denise said it, it was true.

Within a few minutes, they'd narrowed their choices down to sixteen possibilities. So they spent the next half hour in the dressing room, making piles of *no* and *maybe*.

"The saleslady gave me a dirty look the last time I went to get another shade of T-shirt," Jen told Denise conspiratorially. "I'm not sure I blame her, either."

They carefully folded the *no*s so the saleslady wouldn't hate them forever. "I'd better make up my mind now; we're running out of time."

"We are?" Jen asked.

"Yes, we have one other stop to make that I forgot to tell you about: We have to go to Frank's Sporting Goods. Tony needs a new pair of ski goggles. Do you mind?"

"Oh, no," Jen said. She didn't mind at all. She liked doing things for Denise's brother, Tony. He was two years older than Denise and probably the best-looking boy in the high school. He'd found Jen's warmth and understanding wonderful when he'd needed a friend after his latest romance had broken up. The trouble was that Jen had mistaken his friendship for love. It had been hard to accept his explanation that they were just friends . . . good friends. But now she had reluctantly gotten used to it.

Quickly the girls made their decision. Denise bought a white T-shirt with blue polka dots on it and a matching jumbo jean jacket. Even though Jen hadn't *thought* she'd needed anything, she bought a set of multicolored hair bows that Denise said would look pretty on her smooth black hair.

Happily lugging their bags, they headed for Frank's Sporting Goods. They had fifteen minutes until their bus. If they missed that, it would be a half hour until the next one — and Jen would be later than she'd promised Jeff Crawford, the Mann's housekeeper.

Everybody and everything was going crazy at Frank's — particularly Frank. It took Denise ten minutes just to ask for the goggles, and it took Frank another ten to find them in the stock room. While Jen and Denise waited, they looked around the usually orderly store. Every counter was littered with items that should have been put away. Empty boxes lay on the floor, instead of in garbage cans. Clothes that people had tried on, but hadn't bought, were hanging all over or were just lying on top of exercycles and workout benches and weight racks.

By the time Frank appeared with Tony's goggles, most of the other customers had left in disgust.

"I don't believe this," Frank moaned, as he began writing up the slip for Denise.

"You had a cyclone in here?" Jen asked.

"It's my son, Albert — you know him?"

Sure, they knew him. Albert was in the ninth grade. He was one of the school's best students. Everybody admired him because he was so organized. She couldn't believe he would have made such a mess.

"I can't *believe* Albert did this . . ." Jen began.

"Oh, no. That's not it at all. He's in the hospital. Had his appendix out. I never knew how much I counted on him. He's here every day after school and on weekends, pitching in. Now, he's not and it's a disaster. He'll be fine. That's the main thing, I know. But, for another three weeks, I'm in trouble!"

Denise looked at Frank thoughtfully. He was in trouble. He needed help. He needed somebody who could do all the things his orderly fourteen-year-old son did. Why not me? Denise said to herself. She had a sudden image. She could see herself tidying up after customers, finding ski goggles, fishing lures, hunting knives. Demonstrating tennis rackets, assembling sporty jogging outfits. Nothing to it.

"I'll help," she said. "Until Albert's out of the hospital, I'll come here every day after school and do everything Albert did."

Jen almost made the mistake of bursting into laughter, but something in the tone of Denise's offer to Frank stopped her. She and Frank both stared at Denise. Frank spoke first. "Rich girl like you?" he huffed. "What do you need with a job?"

It was the red flag in front of the bull. "I'm not doing it for money," she told him. "I'm just saying I'll help you out because you need help!"

"I'll be okay," he assured her. "You stay home and do your homework. Polish your nails a pretty color," he said.

Jen could tell from Denise's expression that her feelings were hurt. She could also tell that Denise was about to give Frank an argument that he was too tired to hear.

She was trying to do something useful, something meaningful, and it wasn't fair that the man didn't think he needed her. "C'mon, Denise," Jen urged her. "We're going to have to run for the *late* bus now."

Reluctantly, Denise followed her.

Chapter 3

The next day, just as Nora had promised herself, she had gotten to the biology lab early.

She sighed and took the slide out of her microscope. It seemed that no matter where she looked on it, she couldn't find anything. The instructions had said that the water would be loaded with one-celled animals.

"Maybe they're just shy," she reasoned, laughing to herself. The other possibility, of course, was that her experiment was a total failure. She didn't really want to consider that. While she prepared a new slide, she noticed that the science room was stuffy. She opened the window and took a deep breath of the morning air. It was twenty minutes to the first bell, and she'd already been studying for an hour.

Determined, she took the new slide back to the microscope and resumed her search. She didn't mind, really. She knew that doctors had to spend a long time looking for an answer to a complex medical problem. They had to have patience, or they'd lose patients, as she'd read somewhere. Just at that moment, a paramecium swam into sight. She grabbed a pencil and began drawing. Then a second one joined the first on Nora's slide. She was gleeful.

Outside, just beyond the open window of the biology lab, the eighth-graders were gathering on the steps of the school. It was a tradition at Cedar Groves that the eighth grade mobbed the school steps until the first bell rang. It was the time of day when gossip traveled the fastest because they were all together. In the bio lab, Nora *knew* that gossip was traveling — a lot of it — because the buzz was so loud.

She didn't pay much attention, though. She was more concerned about the cluster of paramecia than she was about her classmates. Until she heard her name, and then Jen's.

The person speaking was Susan Hillard. Nora knew she couldn't be saying anything nice about her because she never said anything nice about *anybody*. Susan was telling somebody about Jason's karate demonstration at lunch and how Nora and Jen had stood up for Jason so determinedly.

". . . And then, the two of them started saying how *wonderful* Jason Anthony was.

Can you imagine? I think they really *like* him. I mean, like, a *lot*."

Suddenly, Nora felt like she had a bowling ball in her stomach and her face felt hot — flushed with embarrassment.

"Of all the nerve!" she hissed, ready to jump up and yell out of the window at Susan. Then Mitch Pauley spoke.

"Yeah, I forgot, but Jason was really cool yesterday, wasn't he," he said.

Susan made a sound, something like "Hmmmph!" and walked off.

Nora giggled. She was laughing at Susan for being so silly, and she was laughing at herself for thinking anybody would ever believe Susan. Nora couldn't wait to tell the news to Jen.

She looked back at the microscope. Where, a moment ago, there had been two large paramecia, there were now one large and two little ones. It had multiplied — or divided — and she'd missed it!

Steve stood outside the school with the others, but he really wasn't part of the gossip that morning. He had something else on his mind: Jennifer Mann. He had hardly slept at all the night before, thinking about the years he'd known Jennifer and how now, all of a sudden, he felt he didn't know her at all.

Steve noticed the open window of the

biology lab. It was unusual for a window to be open before school. He looked in. There, on a lab stool, was Nora Ryan, totally concentrating on her microscope. Her mouth was slightly open, soft lips curved into an O. Her brown hair curled around her face. The bright fluorescent lights struck the curls, almost making a halo. She was so pretty that Steve practically gasped. When Nora turned to write in the notebook nearby, he could see the delicate angle of her wrist and her long fingers — surgeon's hands, she called them. It was Nora — the same friend he'd always known, but was it? Suddenly, a new wave broke under his heart and he was struck with realization: He was in love! — with Nora!

And then the first bell rang. Nora put her papers away, closed her notebook, and put the slide in the sink. She turned out the light in the lab and headed for her locker.

Steve walked into the school like an automaton, unsure of anything anymore. Nora . . . Jen . . . Nora.

Nora took her history book and a copy of *Jane Eyre* from her locker. She wasn't paying much attention to what she was doing, though. She was mostly interested in seeing Jen. Where *was* she? Then she saw a flash of bright pink. The exact color of Jen's corduroy jumper. In seconds, the flash arrived at the locker next to Nora's. Skidding to a stop and out of breath, Jen fumbled with the combination lock.

"Hundred-yard-dash tryouts?" Nora asked her.

"Something like that," Jen said, laughing because she knew how silly she must have looked. "I forgot to set my alarm so I missed the bus and then Jeff drove me to school, but the car wouldn't start — you know what it's like, don't you?"

Nora nodded.

Jeff was Jeff Crawford, the Mann's housekeeper. The Mann's had had a live-in housekeeper ever since Jen's mother died when she and her brother, Eric, were little. Jeff was a part of the family now. They loved him and he loved them.

"Jen, you're going to explode when I tell you what *I* overheard this morning! I heard Susan tell Mitch that we thought Jason was *wonderful* and that we really liked him a lot." She mimicked Susan's voice.

"I don't believe her! No one will believe her," Jen said as they began walking toward their first class. They giggled.

"Nora," Jen said, glancing at her friend's books. "Are you reading *Jane Eyre* in French?" Nora looked confused.

"Our first class is French, and you're carrying a history book and *Jane Eyre*."

"What a morning," Nora moaned. "I miss a paramecium reproducing, and now I've got the wrong books. Put a sign on my seat so I can find it, will you?" she asked, turning back to her locker.

"Sure," Jen agreed, smiling. "Anytime."

Chapter 4

Denise got off the bus at the mall. She was alone. She hadn't come to shop. She hadn't come to be with friends or to hang out. She'd come because she wanted to Make a Difference.

Determined, she walked straight to Frank's Sporting Goods.

Just like the day before, Frank was very busy. Stepping into the store, she saw the same chaos. She was sure that some of the jogging suits dangling off the rowing machine in the corner had been there overnight. She was even more certain she was doing a Good Thing.

She'd have to wait for a long time to get Frank's attention. So, she didn't wait. While he helped customers, she put her books and purse behind the counter and began picking up discarded clothing. At first, it was pretty hard to tell what to do with it, but soon she'd figured out that the racks were divided by sport — so that swimming suits did not mix with boxing shorts, even though they looked alike.

She hung up the jogging outfits, and she put the loose basketballs back into the bin. There was a stack of tennis ball cans which had collapsed. She restacked the display into the shape of a pyramid. Then she turned her attention to the fishing rods. They were in a terrible tangle. Although she had no idea what order they should be in, she knew they shouldn't be crisscrossed. She straightened them.

Then suddenly the store was empty, and Frank had a chance to look up from the cash register. His jaw dropped. He couldn't believe what he was seeing as he surveyed his shop. His eyes lighted on Denise.

"You were serious, weren't you?" he asked.

She nodded eagerly.

"Start Monday," he told her. She grinned proudly. "And, uh, thank you," he said.

"You won't be sorry," Denise said. She practically floated to the bus stop, totally unaware of how tired she was. She only felt happy.

Jen and Nora sat on the wooden bench in front of the school. The long day was over and neither of them had to hurry home.

"Nora, I got this neat thing," Jen said, fishing in her purse to bring out the nail polish sampler she'd bought at Bradley's.

Nora looked at it and grinned. She loved to experiment with makeup, though her mother didn't always approve.

"It only cost a dollar," Jen told her. "See, here's Cotton Candy, Roaring Red, Iridescent Ice and — hey, there's Steve!"

"I haven't talked to him all day," Nora said, waving to him.

"I tried to," Jen said, "but he was sort of walking around in a daze."

"Wonder if he's coming down with something," Nora said in her doctor's voice.

Steve looked up. When he saw the girls, his face broke into a silly grin, but he walked past them into the school.

"He's got a Pep Committee meeting now," Jen remembered.

"Doesn't look very peppy to me."

Jen returned her attention to the nail polish. "Next comes Rose Revelry and then Flaming Fire."

"Sometimes I can't believe how dumb the names are for colors of makeup. I mean what other kind of fire is there besides Flaming Fire?"

"Smoldering Fire?" Jen suggested.

Nora poked Jen in the arm. "Look! Jason — on foot." It was unusual to see him off his skateboard.

"Hi, Jason," Nora called out when he came closer.

"Oh, hi, Nora," he said.

"Something happen to your skateboard?" she asked, pointing to the board tucked under his arm.

"Yeah," he held it out. "One of my screws got loose."

Jen and Nora giggled, and Jason joined them. He sat down on the bench next to Jennifer and stared at the wobbly mechanism on the bottom of his skateboard. He wiggled it until he found the loose screw, and then he fished a dime out of his pocket and tried to use it to tighten the screw. It didn't work.

"Here, I've got something that might do it," Jennifer said. She offered Jason a nail file. He took it and studied it as if he'd never seen one before. Then he grasped it firmly and slipped it into the slotted head of the screw and began turning. They were all silent until Jason smiled.

"It works?" Nora asked.

"It works," Jason announced, as he continued fixing his skateboard.

"Gee, Jason," Nora said. "We were pretty impressed with your karate yesterday."

"You were?" he asked, surprise in his voice.

"Sure, we were. We never knew you were so good at it," Jen added.

"I am?"

"Now don't be modest," Nora said.

"Oh, no. I won't do that," he told the girls.

"Have you been studying long?" Jen asked.

Jason stopped his repair work for a minute, as if he were trying to remember how long he'd been studying karate. "Not too long," he said, returning to his work.

"Black belt?" Jennifer asked.

"Oh, sure," he told her, shrugging humbly as if it wasn't important.

"Wow," Nora said. All of a sudden, Nora became aware that she and Jennifer were discovering a part of Jason that nobody had known existed before.

It could change his life.

Everybody had always thought that Jason was just creepy Jason. Now everybody would be able to see a different Jason. They'd see an all-powerful, skillful, deft, and deadly Jason Anthony.

"Is it really true that when you have a black belt, you have to register your hands as a deadly weapon with the police?" Jen asked.

Jason gulped and nodded.

"Must have been scary," Jen said.

"Oh, a little bit," he told them.

"Have other scary things happened?" Jen asked.

"Well, uh, oh, I don't know. But sure," Jason said, unsurely.

"Are you being modest again?" Nora said, encouraging him to speak.

Jason finished working on the skateboard and handed the nail file back to Jennifer. He spun the newly repaired wheels with his dirty hands. Once he was satisfied that the skateboard was working right, he leaned back on the bench and began talking.

"Registering my hands was nothing compared to the last tournament. I won so many ribbons, they had to give me a trophy case to go with it."

"Really?"

"Would I lie?" he asked defensively.

At another time, Nora and Jennifer would have remembered that Jason was perfectly capable of lying — or stretching the truth beyond recognition, anyway. But right then, that wasn't what they were thinking of. They were thinking about how they'd discovered this unknown talent of Jason Anthony's. Susan's putting them down for thinking Jason was wonderful would be laughable if Jason *was* good at karate. So, Jason *had* to be.

"Tell us more," Nora urged him.

"If you really want to hear it. . . ." They nodded. Jason warmed up to his subject. He told them about his last tournament, and the one before it. He leaped to his feet.

"I won the last tournament with a kick like *this*!" he said, jerking his left foot around. "The guy before that got kayoed with a punch!" He shot his right fist straight at them, startling both girls. "I've never lost a match — or a lighter," he joked. Jen and Nora laughed. "See, I may be small, but I've studied for years, learning how to use the weight I have to its best advantage." Jen and Nora hung on every word.

"Where are all these tournaments?" Jen asked.

"Oh, here and there. Not too many here, though," he said, quickly correcting himself. "I mean karate really isn't available in Cedar Groves. There's no *dojo* here, you know what I mean?"

"You mean a Japanese restaurant?" Jen asked.

"No, a karate training gym," he explained.

"Oh, so you do your training out of town," Nora said.

"*Far* out," Jason told them.

Suddenly, Jen remembered something "You know, Jason, I'm not sure you're right." He looked offended, but she went on. "Jeff Crawford was telling me about this friend of his from the army who's working at the Y. His name is Doc Holloway. They called him Doc because every time he got into a fight, the other guy had to go to the doctor. That's why I remembered his name. Anyway, Doc is teaching karate at the Y here in Cedar Groves. There must be some tournaments here. You could enter them, and then you wouldn't have to travel so far out of town for competitions. Wouldn't that be great?" she asked.

"Oh, I don't know," Jason said hesitantly.

"Sure, it would be great," Nora encouraged him.

"But I wouldn't want to show up the other kids, you know?" he said.

"The other kids *need* to be shown up, Jason. You should call the Y right away and find out," Jen said.

"Yeah," Nora added.

"I'll think about it," Jason said. Then he stood up and put his left foot onto his skateboard. He pushed off with his right foot. While Jen and Nora watched, the skateboard, and Jason, were lifted completely off the ground. To their astonishment, it flew into the air while Jason did an airborne turn of 180 degrees, and then brought the skateboard, and himself, back down to the ground upright.

"He's something, you know?" Jen remarked, staring at Jason's receding back.

"Yes, but what?" Nora asked.

All during the Pep Committee meeting, Steve was distracted, just as he had been all day. His mind was jumping back and forth between thoughts of Jen and thoughts of Nora. Love was supposed to be wonderful. This was awful. He was in love with two girls who were best friends with each other and who were supposed to be his best friends, too. How could that happen?

"And, Steve, how much crepe paper do we have left from the Homecoming float?" Somebody asked him. But he didn't hear.

He *couldn't* be in love with two girls at once. He had to be in love with just one of them. So, which one?

Was it Nora, with her curly brown hair and big brown eyes?

"Say, Steve, we're having a meeting here. The subject is crepe paper."

Or was it Jen, who had smooth black hair and hazel eyes and a smile that danced in his heart?

"You remember the stuff, Steve — the colored crinkly paper that we use to make pom-poms?"

He couldn't decide which girl. Only time would tell.

Suddenly, somebody took his hand. "Steve, we're having a meeting. Would you care to beam down?" the chairman asked.

"Meeting?" He repeated numbly and then came to his senses. The rest of the committee members started laughing. "I guess my mind was somewhere else," he admitted.

"Like Mars," the chairman said. Then she spoke to the rest of the committee. "Look, since we don't seem to be able to decide about the pep rally, why don't we just table the discussion and let nature take its course. In another couple of weeks, we'll know more. We can decide then. Everybody agree?" Everybody agreed. Including Steve, though he had no idea what he'd agreed to.

That's the right thing to do, he thought. I'll just let nature take its course and decide later which girl I'm in love with — Nora or Jen, or Jen or Nora.

The meeting was adjourned.

Chapter 5

Jen stood in front of the mirror in Denise's bedroom, trying to put on makeup for Lucy's party. It was more fun getting ready together than alone. Besides, Jen always liked an excuse to be at Denise's house. There was always a chance she'd see Tony.

"Urghhh!" she declared.

"That sounded like an unhappy sound," Denise said.

"It was the sound of me applying mascara to my cheek. I look like a boxer — the one who lost the fight!"

"Here, I'll help you," Denise offered. She came over to the mirror and helped wipe away the mess.

"You know, you wear makeup so naturally. Every time I try to put on anything more than lip gloss and a touch of mascara, I look like I'm on my way to join the circus

— the clown act, if you know what I mean."

"One of the models for Dad's cosmetic company taught me how to put on professional makeup when I was a child," Denise said.

For fifteen minutes, Denise carefully put things from ten different bottles and tubes on Jen's face. Suddenly, her nose, which had always seemed a touch on the big side to Jen, was just exactly right.

"It looks terrific," Jen said, admiring the subtle way Denise had blended the colors. "Only trouble is that I'll have to spend as much money on makeup now as I have on nail polish." She displayed her hand for Denise's admiration. She'd decided on Cotton Candy because it matched the polka dots on her favorite bow.

She and Denise stood side by side, combing their hair.

"Say, what's the stuff I heard about you and Nora and Jason?" Denise asked.

"Oh, Susan, Lady Bigmouth! Nora overheard her talking to Mitch. She's something. . . ." Jen told Denise about Susan's spreading the word that she and Nora were crazy about Jason. As she talked, Jen pulled her hair up on top of her head, holding it up with her hands. "What do you think?" she asked.

Denise tilted her head and studied the

look. "It's not you," she said. "You need something simpler — "

"That's me, a simpleton," Jen said.

"That's not what I meant. It's just that you're so straightforward that a fancy hairdo like that doesn't fit your personality. Here, I've got an idea." Denise took a brush and began styling Jen's hair. She brushed the top straight back off her face, then she swept up the hair at the sides, meeting at the top of Jen's head in a clip. Jen's eyes glowed as she watched Denise work. Finally, Denise topped it off with the pink polka dot bow.

"It looks terrific!" Jen said.

"And terrific suits you," Denise said, turning her attention to her own hair.

"You know, Jen, telling people Jason was wonderful was doing a good thing. Jason needs friends and you're always there when somebody needs a friend, Jen. Always."

Jen understood that Denise was still hurt by Tracy's thoughtless words the other day about her being a millionaire. It seemed funny that somebody who had so much should want something Jen had, but Denise was obviously serious about it. Somehow, Denise was feeling useless.

"And you're always there when I need help with makeup and clothes, Denise."

"Well, you're going to have to help me

with clothes now, because I can't get this necklace fastened."

Jen slipped her pink and blue top over her head, being careful not to muss her makeup or hair. "Just a sec," she said, smoothing out the wrinkles. Then she turned to Denise and fastened the delicate gold chain of her locket.

"Oh, drat!" Jen said.

"Break a nail?"

"No, I just made a scratch in the Cotton Candy polish — "

A few minutes later, they were ready. Jen and Denise stood in front of the full-length mirror and smiled happily at what they saw.

There was a knock at Denise's door and Tony came in. His eyes lighted up and he grinned broadly when he saw the girls. He whistled.

"You both look wonderful!" he said. "This must be some party — wish I'd gotten an invitation." Jen's heart skittered. Suddenly, she realized she could invite Tony to the party. He could come with her, be her date. Maybe they'd dance together, talk, share a snack. Jen was about to open her mouth when her eyes caught Tony's. The look on his face was *very* brotherly and not at all boyfriendly. She'd had her crush on him, but it was over. They were just friends now, she reminded herself firmly. "Boy, I wish *my* brother would say I looked wonderful," she said, instead of asking him to the party. "*My* brother calls me mud-face, not 'wonderful.'"

Tony laughed, that delicious, warm laugh Jen loved. "Your brother needs glasses," he assured her. "Say, can I give you girls a lift to the party?" he offered. He didn't have to ask twice.

Nora stood near the living room entrance at Lucy's house. The living room was filled with people, but she felt very alone. She never had any trouble talking with her friends at school — why should it be difficult just because they were all at a party?

She glanced around the room nervously, hoping nobody was watching her. She spotted Lucy standing across the room, near the stereo. She was looking uncomfortable, too. She was twirling the curls of her short Afro cut with her left hand, while pretending to read an album cover. It made Nora feel better to know that even Lucy, who was the hostess, was a little uncomfortable, too. Nora walked over to her and offered to help choose records. Lucy agreed readily, happy to have someone standing with her.

"I love your dress," Nora told Lucy. She was wearing a straight skirt and a boxy overblouse in a bold print pattern of earth colors.

"Thanks. Mom and Dad brought this material back from Arizona last year. Isn't it neat?" Nora nodded. It was. Lucy's mother was a travel agent, and their family went on a lot of trips.

"Where is your mother?"

"In the kitchen," Lucy told her. "She's making some snacks."

"Maybe I could help her," Nora said, hoping for an excuse to do something.

"Don't bother," Lucy told her. "I already tried that. Mom shooed me out here. Let's hunt for the new Trilogy album together."

"Okay!" Nora agreed — Trilogy was one of her favorite groups.

Just then, Jen and Denise arrived.

While Denise took over the job of choosing record albums with Lucy, Jen and Nora sat on the sofa together to talk. Jen wanted to tell Nora everything Denise had showed her about makeup. Nora agreed that Jen's nose looked smaller.

"But I don't agree with you that it *ever* looked too big," Nora said, annoyed that Denise's knowledge of makeup meant so much to Jen.

Nora's eyes were traveling around the room. Suddenly, Nora looked down. Something, or someone, had caught her looking.

Jen glanced over her shoulder. It was Brad Hartley.

"He's coming over here now, Nora," Jen whispered.

"Dance?" Brad said to Nora. She nodded, smiling, and stood up to dance with him. He led her to the center of the room.

Jen leaned back in the sofa and watched. She felt a little bad, sitting on the sofa while her best friend danced with a handsome boy. She didn't want to dance with Brad because he was Nora's friend, but she wouldn't mind having her own boyfriend. She was about an inch and a half from feeling sorry for herself, when she decided that was silly and stopped watching the dancers.

Jen waved to Steve Crowley as she went to see if Mrs. Armanson could use any help with the food. Steve took a soda from the table and stood in a corner near where Mitch and Tommy were betting with each other about who would be the first to ask Denise to dance. It seemed very babyish to Steve — not like real love at all.

He watched the dancers, a little upset that Nora was dancing with Brad. Well, he couldn't blame her. She didn't know yet that he, Steve, was in love with her. And Jen. There was Jen. She was carrying a tray of little sandwiches. Steve smiled to himself. It was just like Jen to find a way to be helpful. She put the tray on the table, and when Mrs. Armanson told her she didn't need any more help, Jen sat on the sofa by herself. Steve went over to her.

"Would you like to dance?" he asked nervously.

"Oh, hi, Steve. Uh, no thanks," she said. Dancing would be nice, but dancing with Steve would be like dancing with her brother. It wasn't what she needed at that moment. "Come, sit down with me," she invited. He joined her.

Just then, Nora came and sat down, too, on the other side of Steve. He could feel himself shivering with excitement and fear. He'd never known he could feel this way. It was wonderful. It was awful. He felt a real urge to say something. He was pretty sure they would understand. But right then, they seemed almost unaware of him. It seemed funny, since he was aware of nothing *but* them. They were talking about the movie *Jane Eyre*. A revival of it was playing at the Art Theatre, and they were talking about going. Then they started talking about Jason Anthony.

"You know, Denise told me she thinks we did a good thing," Jen told Nora.

"Maybe," Nora said. "Sometimes I think Jason just acts like a jerk because he's not sure of himself."

"That's the thing, you see," Jen said. "If he were more sure of himself, he'd stop acting like a baby. I'm sure that if everybody knew about his black belt, they'd feel differently about him, and then he'd feel differently about himself. Then he wouldn't act so strangely."

"Talking about acting strangely," Jen said, and then tilted her head toward Steve.

Nora had to agree. Steve *had* been behaving very oddly for several days — in fact, ever since right after the Jason Anthony Karate Demonstration.

Nora took Steve's right hand. He felt a delicious chill. Jen took his left hand. Suddenly he was bathed in warmth.

"What's going on, Steve?" Nora asked in the voice she used when she practiced being a doctor in front of the mirror.

"Does your new and odd personality have anything to do with Jason?"

Steve was quiet for a minute. He was trying to think why they would think his behavior could be connected to Jason. In a way, it was. It was after Susan had told him how the girls had defended Jason that he'd discovered how he felt about them. "Yes, it has to do with Jason . . . in a way." He nodded.

"So?" Nora urged him on.

Suddenly, the floodgates opened, and Steve started talking, grasping each of their hands tightly. They both listened very carefully, but they couldn't make much sense out of what he said.

"I can't believe how things change when people get to be teenagers!" he said. "I mean first somebody is just a friend, then all of a sudden there's something more than friendship. It's deeper, it's more serious. It's something more real, even when it's not real. You know what I mean?"

"I think you're saying something," Jen said. "But I'm not sure I know what it is."

"Well, it all started with Jason," Steve said evasively.

Jen leaned forward to listen carefully. Nora, on the other side of Steve, did the same. They didn't want to miss a word.

"Jason?" Jen said, trying to get Steve to say more.

"Yes, Jason. What you did for him in the lunchroom changed all feelings of friendship from casual to, well, something more." He gulped. "To love." It had been hard for him to say it. He waited for the girls to be upset. They weren't.

"Jason?" Nora asked, perplexed.

"That's what started it," Steve said.

"In love with one of us?" Jen asked. She wanted to be sure she understood. Steve nodded.

"Which one?" Nora asked.

"I don't know," Steve said desperately.

"That's what makes it so hard. But as soon as I know, I'll tell you. I promise." He stared ahead, embarrassed by his confession. "I've got to go now." He jumped up and disappeared onto the boys' side of the room.

Nora and Jen didn't have a chance to speak to him again at Lucy's party. They didn't even have a chance to speak to each other again. Just about then, the party warmed up. It was as if everybody figured out at the same moment that the kids at the party were the same kids who were at school all day long, and just because they were at a party didn't mean they had to be uptight.

Chapter 6

"And then, Lucy had this contest where we got to see if we could name the group while she played the record. She had some pretty weird albums, I'll tell you," Nora said, leaning back on her pillow, which was propped up against the wall. Her sister, Sally, sat on the foot of her bed, arms circling her legs. It was Saturday morning. Nora was wearing her favorite fuzzy bathrobe and telling Sally about Lucy's party.

"I tried that at a party here a couple of years ago," Sally said. "Nobody could get any of the groups, either, because I went into Mom's old record collection. I stumped them with The Kingston Trio. Sounds like yours was a good party."

"Oh, it was," Nora sighed, remembering how she'd danced with Brad. "Except for one thing. Steve Crowley was really weird. Listen, I promise to explain biology to you if you'll explain boys to me — "

It sounded like a good deal to Sally, since she had a biology test on Monday. Nora told her everything she could remember from the weird conversation she and Jen had with Steve.

"I don't get it," Nora said. "What was he talking about? And why was he so upset? I mean, he could barely talk to us afterward."

"It's pretty obvious to me," Sally said. "He'd just learned from Jason that the guy's fallen for you both. Steve was upset because he's afraid that one of you is going to feel jealous of the other. He's a really good friend, see, and he wouldn't want that to happen."

"Think so?" Nora asked dubiously.

"I *know* so," Sally assured her. "Now tell me the difference between mitosis and meiosis."

"Oh, that's *easy*," Nora began. It was easier than thinking about Jason Anthony being in love with her.

Jen and Nora stood in the line at the movie theater where *Jane Eyre* was playing. Most of their English class was there, too. Mr. Rochester had asked them to see the movie, and since that seemed easier than wading through the book, a lot of them were doing it.

While Jen and Nora traded stories

about Lucy's party, Jason Anthony rolled by.

He didn't see them. As far as Nora was concerned, it was just as well.

"You're not going to believe this, Jen," she said, watching Jason tic-tack down the sidewalk on his skateboard.

"I talked with Sally about our conversation with Steve," Nora told her. "Sally thinks Jason's in love with both of us, and Steve's upset because he thinks we're going to be jealous of each other."

Jen just stared. "That's ridiculous! Jealous because of Jason!" she burst out laughing.

Tracy Douglas came up behind them in line, as Nora and Jen were hanging on to each other laughing. Tracy was the most boy-crazy girl in their class. Sometimes it seemed to Jen and Nora that Tracy had discovered boys while they were just learning to read.

"There you are!" Tracy said, joining Jen and Nora. "Guess who I just saw? Jason Anthony," she said, answering her own question. "Susan Hillard told me what you guys did for him. You must be *crazy* about him!"

It was probably just coincidence. What else could explain why everyone was beginning to think that Jen and Nora and

Jason were in some kind of love triangle?

"Oh, groan," Nora said.

"What's the matter?" Tracy asked her.

Nora and Jen exchanged glances to see if they were ready to share the information Steve had given them. Jen shrugged her shoulders. "Maybe Tracy has some insight into this situation, right?" Nora agreed.

"Well, Tracy, you're a real expert in these things, so maybe you can help us. We *think* Steve told us last night that Jason is in love with one of us but can't decide which one. Could that be?"

Tracy blinked her eyes in thought. Then she nodded. "I think so," she said. "I remember one time when I thought I was in love with one of two guys, but I couldn't decide which one it was."

"Tell me about it," Nora said, suddenly interested.

"Well, there was this one class, and every time I went to it, I'd get this funny queasy feeling in my stomach. Since I always sat between two particular guys, I was sure it meant that I was in love with one of them."

"So, which was it, and how did you figure it out?" Jen asked.

"Actually, it turned out that I wasn't in love with either of them. The class was biology, and I figure it was the formaldehyde that was giving me the queasy stomach," Tracy told them.

For a second, Jen and Nora stared at Tracy. They were wondering if she were for real. At the same instant, all three of them started giggling.

"That's not real helpful," Nora said.

"I know, but it happened," Tracy said seriously.

Jen's eyes were on the screen in the movie, but her mind was on Steve Crowley and Jason Anthony. She remembered how she felt when Nora was dancing with Brad at Lucy's house. She wanted to have a boyfriend. She wanted to have dates. Jason Anthony probably wouldn't have been her first choice, but he was sweet and, after all, there was his karate skill. His red hair was kind of cute, too, she thought. At first, the idea of Jason being interested in her had been awful, but maybe it wouldn't be as awful as she first thought.

But how did Nora feel about this? She'd have to wait to find out.

That night Nora picked up the phone and dialed Jen's number. It was nine o'clock. They talked to each other absolutely every night between eight and nine o'clock except when one of them wasn't home. Some nights they talked for a long time. Some nights they just spoke long enough to compare what they planned to wear the next day.

Nora waited while Jen's phone rang twice. They'd left each other right after the movie because Jen was rushing off to Denise's house, but Nora was sure Jen would be home by now. The phone rang a third time — then a fourth. Then the phone was picked up. Nora waited for Jen's familiar "Hello." It didn't come.

There was an "Aaargh," followed by a "Yikes!" followed by an earsplitting *THUNK!* Then there was a peculiar progression of grunts and strange scraping sounds.

"Jen, are you there? Can you hear me? Is everything okay?" The grunts and scraping sounds continued. Nora became convinced that something terrible was going on. Maybe Jen's house had been robbed and her hands and feet were tied. Nora had an image of Jen trying to talk in spite of the gag. Just before Nora decided to race over to Jen's house, she heard a clear, familiar voice.

"I don't believe this!"

"Jen? What's going on there?"

"I knew it was you," Jen said.

"Are you okay?"

"Sure, if you think ten nails with smudged polish is okay."

Nora giggled. "You just finished putting the polish on when the phone rang. Right? Then you dropped the phone when you tried to pick it up with your wrists — "

"Feet — " Jen corrected her.

"And the phone slid under the bed."

"You got the picture, all right," Jen said glumly.

Jen examined the damaged nails carefully. She tucked the phone firmly between her chin and her shoulder and began to redo the polish. This time, she'd chosen Iridescent Ice.

Nora said, "I've been thinking about Jason."

"Me, too," Jen said.

"Listen, he's really kind of sweet, and if he wants to be my boyfriend, it's okay with me," Nora confessed.

"What about Brad?" Jen asked her.

"Brad isn't *really* a *boyfriend*. Not exactly a serious one, anyway. He's just somebody who's going to ask me out every once in a while," Nora said. "I don't think that makes him a real boyfriend yet. Of course, Jason isn't, either. Yet."

"Okay," Jen said. "I've been thinking about this, too, and I agree that going out with Jason would be okay. There's something neat about a guy who's a karate black belt."

"Yeah," Nora said dreamily.

"But we don't know which one of us he's in love with," Jen reasoned. "What are we going to do about that?"

"Well . . . you and I should both be nice to him — kind of let him know we'd be interested, if he is. And then, we'll let nature take its course. Sooner or later, Steve or Jason will let us know which one he's chosen. I promise if it's you, my feelings won't be hurt."

"I promise the same thing," Jen said.

There was a moment of silence on the telephone. Jen blew on her newly polished nails, trying to think of what to say to Nora, her best friend, with whom she'd just made a deal she wasn't sure she could keep.

Chapter 7

On Monday, when Nora finished buying her lunch, she found that the big table in the center of the room where she usually sat was already full of other eighth-graders. There was only one seat in the cafeteria left at a little table for two in the corner. One other person was at it. That person was Jason.

Nora took a deep breath and headed for that table.

"Okay if I sit down?" she asked.

Jason glanced at the food on Nora's tray, not at Nora, shrugged, and said, "Sure."

It occurred to Nora that this was an odd form of behavior for a boy in love, but then Jason was an odd boy. No question about it. Nora sat.

Jason speared a meatball with his fork. Holding it aloft, he began eating it like a candy apple. Nora stared in horror as he turned the fork, munching on the ever-diminishing meatball. Then, when he'd eaten about half of it, he stuffed the rest in his mouth.

Nora opened her container of yogurt and sliced a fresh peach into it.

Jason repeated the candy apple procedure with his next meatball.

Nora mixed the fruit into her yogurt with a teaspoon and took a small bite.

Jason reached for his choco-drink, first blew bubbles into the mixture and then slurped out of the container.

Nora decided that if Jason asked her out, she hoped it wouldn't be for dinner. Then it occurred to her that if she could teach him something about nutrition, he could be an even better athlete than he was. Now, there was a goal worth seeking!

"Jason, you know, a lot of people who study martial arts become interested in Asian nutritional theories."

"They do?" Jason asked, looking uncertain.

"Yes. The Asians have developed many healthy habits, mostly of necessity. Their diets are high in fiber, and low in cholesterol, with few chemicals and processed foods. What *you're* eating is an invitation to clogged arteries and sluggish digestion."

"It is?"

"Yes, it is. You know, if your body isn't working at its peak, it's hard to understand how it can perform at its peak in athletics, such as karate."

"I guess you really know what you're talking about," Jason said. Nora was pleased by his compliment. Then Jason stood up and took his piece of double chocolate layer cake in one hand, his skateboard in the other. He stuffed most of the cake into his mouth all at once. "See you," he said.

He put the skateboard onto the floor and rolled out of the lunchroom before Nora could tell him about the dangers of refined sugar. She decided it was okay, though. There was no way he could learn everything he needed to know about nutrition at once. And he had a lot to learn.

Watching his receding back, she thought he certainly wasn't acting like somebody in love. Shy, she decided. But I'll find a way to bring him out of his shell, she told herself.

That afternoon, Jen had an errand at the copy shop. She'd promised her Save the Whale committee that she'd be in charge of having the handouts duplicated for the next meeting. To remind herself about her errand at the copy shop, Jen wore her sweat shirt which said: EXTINCTION IS FOREVER. It had pictures on it of dodo birds, passenger pigeons, and other extinct species.

Sometimes, Jen couldn't believe how un-informed people were about nature. If the nations of the world weren't careful, whales could become extinct, too. She shivered to think of it and then walked into the shop.

While she waited for the copying to be done, she thought about Denise. She'd had such an odd visit with her on Saturday. The whole time, Denise had talked about how wonderful Jen was since she did so many things for other people. Every time Jen tried to interrupt and suggest something to Denise that she could do, Denise had just smiled mysteriously. Jen knew Denise was up to something. Denise was normally about as mysterious as Jason. Then, Jen realized that might not be a good comparison. Jason did seem fairly mysterious these days.

Jen paid for the copying, put the papers in an envelope, and left the shop. Her next stop was the YMCA, where she had to meet her brother Eric after his woodworking class.

Just as Jen rounded the corner toward the Y, she saw Jason. Once again, he was carrying his skateboard rather than riding it. He walked over to the bench by the bus stop and sat down. Jen decided it was her golden opportunity to have a private talk with him. He seemed completely unaware of her as she walked over and sat next to him.

While she watched, he spun the wheels on his skateboard. They squeaked. He listened. He spun them again. They squeaked again. He stared at the board intently. He scrunched his face in concentration.

"Needs oil," Jennifer said.

"Huh?" Jason responded, surprised to find her next to him.

"The skateboard needs oil. The ball bearings need some lubricant."

"They do?"

At Cedar Groves Junior High School, everybody took industrial arts. Jason had obviously chosen drafting first, before mechanical arts. Jen enjoyed working with motors, engines, and linkages. Anybody could tell when a machine needed oil — anybody except Jason, it seemed.

"Look, Jason, if there is no lubrication, you get a squeak. Ever hear of squeaky wheels?" He nodded sheepishly. "That's what you've got. So you've got to give it some grease — or really any kind of lubricant will do."

Jason gave her a puzzled look.

"Here," Jen said. "I've got just the thing." She fished in her purse, removing her wallet, her keys, her lipstick, her mascara, a blusher, a pack of gum, a three-week-old note to her father from her gym teacher, a bus transfer, three Q-tips, her nail file, an eyelash curler, two hair bows, and a crumpled tissue. Her cheeks turned bright red as she looked at the pile of junk from her purse. Just as she was about to give up, she found the very thing she'd wanted first.

"Here it is!" she said brightly, trying to pretend she didn't have an incredible stack of junk on her lap. "Look, cuticle oil."

Carefully, Jen put the junk back into her purse, except for the cuticle oil and a Q-tip. She took the skateboard and put it on her lap. She spun the wheels as Jason had done. It wasn't actually the ball bearings that were squeaking, she noticed. It was the front axle. Carefully, she put some cuticle oil on one of the Q-tips and then pressed the cotton against the fitting and turned the wheel slowly, leaving a light coating of oil. She showed Jason how to do it on the other side as well. He followed her instructions, and when he'd finihsed, he spun the wheels. There was a pleasant, faint whirr. No squeak.

"Gee, thanks, Jen," he said, climbing onto the board. "That's great." He pushed off with one foot and rolled away smoothly and swiftly without saying good-bye.

Aside from being embarrassed about all the junk she carried, Jennifer was pleased. She'd been able to help Jason, and he was grateful. He'd thanked her, but he sure had gone away quickly. If that was love, it was very strange.

Shy, she said to herself. He's just shy. She stared after him dreamily. She was thinking too hard about Jason to notice that Steve was coming toward her.

He couldn't believe his good luck. He was on his way to see *Jane Eyre*, which he had to do for his English assignment, and there was Jennifer, one of the two people in the world he most wanted to be with. Maybe she'd go to the movie with him, he thought happily.

"Uh, hi, Jen," he said.

"Oh, it's you!" Jen said, startled from her daydreaming.

"Say, would you like to go to *Jane Eyre* with me? That's where I'm going, and since we have to do it for English — "

"Oh, no, thanks, Steve," Jen said, cutting him off before he could even finish the invitation.

It hurt. Jen obviously didn't want to be with him, even after he'd told her how he felt. "I understand," he said reluctantly, and he ran down the street to the theater. Nora, he thought to himself. It will be Nora, then.

Chapter 8

From the minute Denise had walked into Frank's, the afternoon hadn't been quite what she'd bargained for. For one thing, over the weekend, the place had gotten into an even worse mess than it had been the previous week. But then, when she'd tried to hang up some scattered jogging suits, Frank had yelled at her because she was putting them on the wrong rack. They were men's jogging suits. She was putting them on the women's rack.

Next, he'd asked her to get a fishing knife from the display case. She'd given him a hunting knife. It looked to her like you could cut a fish with it. He'd just tossed it back into the case and gotten the fishing knife himself.

After that, he'd asked her to help a customer who wanted a handball glove. The customer was perfectly happy with the golf glove she'd almost sold him. Frank wasn't.

He'd sighed, just as if he were getting a little tired of Denise. She was determined, though. She was going to be helpful to Frank if it *killed* her.

Right at that moment, it looked as though it might.

While she was putting skis back in their racks by size and brand, she'd overheard Frank with a customer, talking about size thirteen hiking boots. Frank said he didn't have any. But Denise wanted to help. She knew where the hiking boots were stored. They were to the right, in the long narrow back room, stacked up on the shelves that went all the way to the twelve-foot ceiling. She'd watched Frank get things down from the high shelf. She pulled over the tall step-ladder, just as he had done. She climbed up on it, just as he had done.

She spotted hiking boots over to the left. Carefully, Denise climbed down and moved the ladder to the left. She climbed back up again, being very careful not to look down. Twelve feet up from the floor didn't seem like much. Twelve feet down from the ladder was another thing.

Denise's eyes ran over the boxes stacked so high. Eleven, eleven-and-a-half. Twelve. There were two size twelve-and-a-halfs. Briefly, she wondered if the guy would mind scrunching his toes. She decided he would so she kept on looking. Thirteen!

There was one pair. She checked the label again. Definitely right. It was just out of reach to the right. She leaned to the right. A little farther. She stretched. She took her right foot off the ladder and put it on the edge of a shelf. She could reach it! Her fingers grasped at the box, but she couldn't get it. She slid one finger under the edge of the box's lid. She had it. She tugged at the box. It moved. She tugged a little harder. It moved some more. What Denise didn't notice, though, was that all eight boxes on top of it moved as well — to say nothing of the dozen beneath it, and those to the right and left.

Denise yanked the box victoriously out of the shelf. It came out. So did forty-seven other boxes all around it — all tumbling to one gigantic, disastrous mess on the floor.

With mounting horror, she climbed down the ladder to the sea of boots, boxes, and tissue paper. By the time Frank arrived to inspect the disaster, Denise was in tears.

"I was just trying to get the size thirteen hiking boots!" she wailed. "I didn't mean to make such a mess. I'm sorry, and I promise I'll have it cleaned up in just a few minutes. But here are the boots the man wanted," she said, handing Frank the box.

Frank looked at it a little oddly. "He wanted a *children's* size thirteen. We don't carry them. I sent him to Kiddle Foot."

Suddenly Denise was crying uncontrollably.

Ten minutes later, she had stopped crying and was on her way home. Frank had thanked her, but he hadn't seemed really grateful. But then, Denise reasoned honestly, he didn't have much to be grateful about. She'd do better tomorrow, she promised herself.

At the same time Denise was at Frank's, Jen was waiting for her brother. When she'd gotten to the Y, Eric wasn't ready. It seemed to Jen that Eric was *never* ready and that was the problem — one of them anyway — with having a little brother, no matter how close you were to him.

While Eric finished his woodworking project, Jen shifted from one foot to the other and read the notices posted on the bulletin board. One announced a garage sale that had taken place four months ago. Another invited people to join a jewelry class scheduled to begin the week before. One offered baby-sitting services. One welcomed people to the Y's karate program —

"That's it!" Jen exclaimed.

"You say something, Miss?" the man behind the desk asked without looking up from his crossword puzzle.

"No, uh, sorry. I mean, yes. Do you have

a brochure or something about the karate program?"

"Mighty popular these days, karate is. Mighty popular. Here you go." He handed her a sheet of paper.

Just as Jen was about to sit down and read it, Eric appeared, proudly displaying his birdhouse.

"Hey, that's neat," Jen told him, stuffing the karate brochure in her pocket. She'd look at it later when she was alone.

After homework and supper, Jen had her Save the Whales meeting. They'd been working on a letter-writing campaign, and Jen was trying to keep track of the letters written so far.

She'd been so interested in the Save the Whales meeting that she'd almost forgotten about the karate brochure until she sank onto her bed, ready to call Nora.

She felt the wad of paper in her pocket and fished it out of her jeans to read:

STUDY KARATE WITH DOC HOLLOWAY
Learn the ancient art of unarmed
self-defense

The brochure went on to describe how anybody could sign up to learn karate and master the techniques under the careful teaching of Doc Holloway. Once those techniques were mastered, all students were welcome to enter Doc's annual "Karate Kick-Off Open Championship." Anybody could sign up for the competition, even if he or she wasn't Doc's student, the brochure said. It was a tournament of skills, not of combat, testing the students' knowledge and ability in the techniques of the sport, Jennifer read.

Jen pictured Jason in a *gi*, covered with ribbons, which he'd won in the individual events, receiving a gigantic trophy. He was smiling proudly. Jen and Nora stood near him. Most of the eighth-graders were in the stands cheering their heads off. Jen was so happy for Jason that she almost felt a tear forming in her eye.

"Wow!" Jen said aloud to the empty room. "That's it!" It would be the perfect chance for Jason to show everybody his incredible talent. Once everybody saw how good Jason was, they'd stop teasing him and Jason would have more confidence. He wouldn't be so shy anymore. He'd be the eighth-grade hero. And he'd be *her* boyfriend — or Nora's.

There were just two things she had to do. The first was to get him to sign up for the tournament. The second was to be sure the whole class would be there for his moment of triumph. Easy, she said to herself.

Then, sitting up in excitement, she

looked at the brochure again. With a sinking heart, she realized that the deadline for nonstudents to sign was the Saturday before. And the tournament was only two-and-a-half weeks away.

Jen reached for the phone. Nora answered right away, positive proof that *she* hadn't just polished her nails, and Jen told her about Doc Holloway's class and about the Kick-Off, as well as the bad news about the deadline.

"Don't worry about it, Jen," Nora comforted her. "I'm sure Jason knows all about it. After all, he's an expert and there aren't that many around. I'll bet you he's already signed up."

"Think so?"

"I'm almost certain so."

But they weren't so certain the next day.

"Have you seen Jason?" Jen asked Denise on the school steps.

"Don't remember," she said and then left, saying she had to ask Tommy Ryder a question. Jen knew something was bothering Denise. She was behaving very strangely. But at the moment, she didn't have the time to figure it out.

Jen turned around, looking for Jason. Mia Stevens and Andy were behind her. "Have you seen Jason?" Jen asked Mia. Mia and Andy both shook their heads. Since they were wearing matching heavy metal earrings as a part of their his-and-hers punk look, there was an odd sort of clanking sound when they moved.

"Have you seen Jason this morning?" Jen asked Amy Williams.

Amy's brown eyes looked puzzled. "No, I haven't. Nora already asked me the same thing."

"Sorry," Jen said, somewhat embarrassed.

There was no sign of Jason until the last second before the bell rang.

"There he is!" Nora said excitedly, finally spotting Jason's familiar face through the crowd.

"Something's wrong," Jen said immediately, watching him approach the school.

"Yeah," Nora agreed. "He's not riding his skateboard."

"And he looks glum. You know, no matter how irritating he can be, he's usually pretty cheerful."

"Mr. What-Me-Worry," Nora said.

"Hi, Jason," Jen said.

He glanced up at her and walked on silently. Jen wondered if that meant that maybe he'd decided against her in favor of Nora. Nora wondered the same thing.

"Hi, Jason," Nora said.

Jason didn't even look up. He just walked into the school building.

"Say, what's with Jason?" Tracy asked, having seen Jason slide past Jen and Nora.

Nora shrugged.

By lunchtime, almost everybody had noticed that Jason wasn't acting normal — for him.

"When Susan told Mr. Morris that she'd named her amoeba 'Jason,' he didn't even react," Nora told Jen.

"And then after we dissected that clam, I was sure Jason would ask if he could eat it. He didn't," Tommy told the group. "There's definitely something wrong."

It was time for action. Jen stood up from the table and grabbed Nora's sleeve. "Come on," she said. "We've got work to do."

"We do?"

"Yes, we do," Jen said. She spoke with such finality that Nora knew Jen was absolutely determined to do whatever she'd decided to do. Together, they found a quiet corner in the library between Ancient History and Dog Training, where they could talk.

"Maybe it's the tournament," Jen explained, sitting at an old wooden table that had a nubbled feeling from generations of initials being scratched onto it.

"How could it be the tournament? That's not for another two-and-a-half weeks," Nora said.

"Right, but the deadline to sign up was

four days ago. Do you suppose Jason missed it, and he's upset because he can't get into it?"

"Jen, you don't know any of this for sure," Nora said.

"I just have a feeling I'm right. We're going to go to the Y after school and talk to Doc Holloway."

"We are?" Nora asked.

Jen nodded vigorously. Looking at her friend, Nora was a little nervous. Jen's determination was fierce and sometimes blind.

"Okay," Nora agreed nervously. She knew when Jen got like this it was best to just go along with her.

Jen's knees were practically shaking while she talked to Doc Holloway. She felt very small standing in front of him. He was at least six feet tall, with rugged features, and piercing blue eyes. One look at him, and Jen was sure he could chop a person in half with his bare hands — or was that only bricks?

"We have a friend," Jen said. "You see, I think he missed the deadline to sign up for the tournament, but he's really good — "

Doc looked at her skeptically.

" — but he's too shy to come talk to you himself, you see. But he's a black belt and never lost a match. Could you make an exception and let him be in it?"

"Since he's that good, I'm a little surprised I don't know about him already," Doc said.

"Well, he's been keeping his karate a secret," Jen told him.

"Hmmm." Doc sighed. The girls were relieved to see that he was considering their request. Finally, he nodded. "Okay," he said. "I'd like to see this guy. Tell him to be here on the twenty-fourth."

"Oh, thank you!" Jen cried. "You won't be sorry. Jason's terrific!"

"Well, if he's that good, he could probably be an assistant instructor as well. You're doing me a big favor. I think." He shook their hands and they were out of the Y less than five minutes after they'd entered it.

"You know, I think we've done something *wonderful*," Jen said.

"Yeah, I can just see Jason holding the karate trophy triumphantly in one arm," Nora said, standing like the Statue of Liberty to demonstrate. But she didn't sound sure.

"Right, and one of us in the other. . . ." Jen's voice trailed off. The friends regarded each other seriously.

It was a sobering thought.

Chapter 9

Jennifer stood on the steps of the school the next morning. She had arrived early just to be sure to see Jason when he arrived. She couldn't wait to tell him the good news. In the meantime, since Jason was late as usual, she took the opportunity to spread the word to the other eighth-graders.

Mitch, Tommy, and Brad thought the tournament was a great idea and promised to be there. Susan Hillard just gave Jen a withering look. Jen laughed to herself. Mia and Andy, together as usual, hadn't known that Jason's karate was good enough for him to be in a tournament.

"Oh! It's *so* exciting!" Tracy said, hugging Jennifer. She promised to come to the tournament, too. At least half of Jen's daydream about Jason's karate was coming true: The whole class would attend his triumph. But what about Jason? There was still no sign of him. Then Steve appeared.

"Hi!" she said waving excitedly to him in anticipation. Certainly, Steve would be even more excited than their other friends about her plan. He was the only one who knew about how Jason felt about Jen and Nora.

Steve's face lit up when he saw Jen waving to him, and he came over to her side and lingered there, behaving almost like a puppy.

"Want to hear my good news this morning?" she asked excitedly. He nodded. "Jason's going to be in the karate tournament at the Y on the twenty-fourth, she announced.

"He is?"

"Yes, he is."

"Jason?"

"Yes, Jason," Jen said, puzzled by Steve's apparent confusion.

"Karate tournament?" Steve asked.

"Is there an echo around here?" Jen teased.

"Echo?"

"You're hopeless," Jen said in exasperation at his strange behavior. But she did wonder what was causing it. Before she had a chance to ask him, he left, looking concerned. Jen shook her head. She really didn't have time to worry about Steve. She *had* to find Jason.

"What's with Steve?" Nora asked her a

few seconds later. "I just told him about Jason, and he looked like he was going to burst into tears."

"I think I'm going to give up trying to understand the whole human race," Jen said. "Absolutely nobody is behaving normally these days — except you and me."

"Maybe," Nora told her. Jen didn't find that very comforting.

Later, Steve sat in the boys' locker room between his PE and history classes, and moped. He was finding life more and more difficult. It wasn't in the least bit fair that Jen and Nora should both be so interested in Jason. After all, what did Jason have that he didn't have? Revealing his feelings to the girls had taken all his courage, yet all they wanted to do was to talk about Jason. How could it be that the minute he fell in love with two different girls at the . same time, *they* both fell in love with someone else?

Suddenly, there was a loud snapping sound next to Steve. He jumped. It was Tommy Ryder, who had emerged from the shower with a damp towel that he'd snapped loudly on the bench where Steve sat.

"Say, Crowley," Tommy said, demanding Steve's attention. "Did you hear that Denise Hendrix is working at Frank's

Sporting Goods?" Steve shook his head. "Mitch and I are going to stop by there after school and see if they have any new baseballs. Maybe she'll help us. Want to come?"

"No, thanks," Steve said.

"How come all of a sudden all the girls are into sports?" Tommy asked. "I mean what's with your girl friends and this karate thing?"

"Not *my* girl friends," he sighed.

Tommy laughed. "It's no laughing matter," Steve blurted out. "They've both fallen for Jason Anthony."

"Jason?" Tommy said in disbelief. It was true that Tommy couldn't really understand any girl falling for *any* boy but himself, but a *pair* of girls falling for Jason Anthony was almost beyond comprehension.

"Yes, Jason," Steve said. "It seems that Jason's become a karate expert, and Jen and Nora are really interested in him because of it."

"Jen told me about the tournament on the twenty-fourth. When did Jason ever get off his doofus skateboard long enough to learn karate?" Tommy asked.

"Beats me," Steve said. He sighed deeply and then started getting dressed.

In the West Gym, Jen dashed through the door into the girls' locker room. She grabbed Nora by the shoulders while she was trying to put on her sky-blue sweater.

"Nora, he's got laryngitis!" she cried.

"Who? What?" Nora asked, reasonably, straightening out her sweater.

"Jason does! Mitch told me that's why Jason isn't in school today. We didn't even notice it, but he left yesterday afternoon. He was so sick that the nurse sent him home. Isn't that terrible?"

"He'll probably be better in a couple of days," Nora said matter-of-factly. "I had it once. It didn't last much longer than a cold. He'll have to take care of himself, breathe warm, moist air. . . ."

Nora wisely prescribed Jason's cure. Jen pictured the weakened hero propped up against pillows in his bed. Laboriously, he raised a hand in greeting and then smiled, slightly. He was so brave!

"How can you be so matter-of-fact when Jason's so sick?" Jen demanded.

"It's not that big a deal. You feel crummy, you can't talk, but you get better soon," Nora said. She really loved being an authority on things.

"You can't talk?" Jen said, suddenly a little nervous about something.

"Sometimes not as much as a squeak," Nora informed her.

And then, at the same instant, both girls figured it out.

"Oh, no!" Nora moaned, suddenly losing her cool bedside manner.

"Jen, Jason's peculiar behavior yesterday had nothing to do with karate and everything to do with laryngitis. He probably didn't even *know* about the tournament and now he's all signed up for it. I'm getting a *bad* feeling about this," Nora said.

"Oh, come on, Nora. It can't be all that bad. Listen, he'll still thank us for signing him up for it, right?"

"Maybe," was as far as Nora would go.

"So, the thing to do is to let him know what we've done and to make sure he gets better in time. What's the best thing for laryngitis?"

"Chicken soup," Nora told her.

"Give me a break," Jen said.

Nora waited while Jen quickly showered and dressed. They were silent. Jen's mind was filled with images of Jason and how grateful he was going to be to her, and Nora, for what they were doing for him. She was genuinely and deeply worried about him and how sick he was.

Nora was taking a more practical turn. What proof did they have, really, that Jason was a karate expert? Why was Jen so certain that he wanted to be in the dumb tournament? How could it be that all of a sudden, out of the blue, Jason had fallen in love with *both* of them? Nora knew that if she started pressing Jen with these questions, Jen's feelings would be hurt. She didn't want to do that. Jen was her best friend.

"Tell you what, Jen," Nora said. "After school, we'll go to your house and call Jason from there, okay?"

"Okay," Jen agreed. She knew she'd feel a hundred percent better after she'd talked with Jason — or *to* Jason at any rate. She was sure he'd feel a hundred percent better after he knew what they'd gotten him into.

What *had* they gotten him into?

After school that day, Denise took a deep breath to steady herself. After all, she hadn't exactly left Frank's covered in glory the day before. Now she was returning, and she wanted to do the job right. She promised herself she wasn't going to mix up any of the equipment, and she wasn't going to do anything stupid. What a promise! she groaned to herself. But she was serious about helping Frank. She wanted to be helpful to somebody who needed her. She wanted to do it right! She'd even spent time with Mitch, asking him about sports and sports equipment. He'd promised he'd drop by the store, too. He could help her get out of a jam, if she got into one.

"Hi, Frank," she said brightly as she entered the store.

"Well, hello, Denise," he greeted her. "You seem to have some customers waiting for you already."

Denise looked behind him. There were six boys from her class, including Mitch, Tommy, Brad, and Marc Johnson. Frank seemed delighted to have all these customers. Denise could tell that he knew they'd come because she was there, so he'd decided it was a brilliant idea for her to be in the store.

"Say, Denise, we're thinking of going skiing in South America over summer vacation. Have you got any skis that are designed for the Andes?" Tommy asked.

"My old lacrosse stick seems to have got some kind of imbalance," Mitch began. "Do you have a good selection of them?

Before Marc could ask about surfboards, she'd pointed Tommy toward the skis and showed Mitch where the lacrosse sticks were. She only had a second to wonder why on earth Tommy was looking at skis *today*, for a trip that was months away, and why Mitch was looking for a "selection" of lacrosse sticks when the season was over. Never mind, she told herself. Some things in life just *don't* make sense. Boys, she decided, were a prime example.

"What do you think, Denise? The solid blue warm-up suit, or is it better with contrasting top?" Marc asked. When did he change from surfing to running?

"Solid," she said.

"Say, Denise?" Brad called from the dressing room. "Have you got the all-cotton socks in the school colors?"

"I'll check," she said agreeably. But then she paused for a minute. "What are the school colors?" she asked.

Before she could hear his answer, another boy wanted to know if they had any left-handed fishing reels. "I'll check," she told him.

"Denise, can I take the golf cart for a test drive?" somebody she didn't even recognize called out from the far side of the store.

"I'll check," she told him, as she waded through the aisles cluttered with boys from her class, trying to find Frank to ask him all these questions.

"Can you show me a *really* good epée?"

"Huh?"

"You know, for fencing," the boy said.

"Oh." The pronunciation had thrown her off. "No, I can't."

"Well then, how about a fencing mask?"

"I'll check," she said, now getting really irritated. "I've got a million questions," she said to Frank.

"What you really have is a million customers," he said, beaming. Denise was glad to see Frank so happy, but she was getting a funny feeling about these so-called customers. She didn't see any of the boys taking purchases up to the cash register. She did see a lot of them looking at equipment and trying to get *her* attention, not Frank's.

"Say, Denise!" Marc called from the rear of the store. "Can you help me choose a surfboard?"

"Give me a break, Marc!" she yelled back at him.

"Why, Denise," Frank said, surprised. "You shouldn't speak to customers like that. Remember, they are my bread and butter."

"Yes, Frank," she said. What she didn't say was that Marc had been born and brought up in the Big Sur country of California and knew everything there was to know about surfboards. He didn't need her help — at all.

What was going on here? Then Denise remembered the rash of unexplained illness among the male population of the school the day she had been the "nurse," when the eighth grade had run the school. Finally, she'd diagnosed that situation as a case of mass temporary insanity. It seemed to have struck again.

Denise was at her wits' end, though. If she helped the boys, it wouldn't do any good because they weren't going to buy anything anyway. If she didn't help them, Frank would be upset because he didn't see what was really going on.

Well, she decided, it was better for Frank to be angry with the boys than with her.

"Frank," she said. "Have we got any skis designed for the Andes mountains?"

He looked at her very strangely.

Chapter 10

Jen sat on the beanbag chair in her room with her feet propped on a stack of books. She stared at the ceiling. Nora was lying on the floor, tracing circles on the hardwood floor with her fingers. They were both more than a little nervous.

"I talked to Doc. *You* call Jason," Jen declared.

Nora grunted. There was silence for a few minutes.

"You talked to Doc. *You* call Jason," Nora countered.

"Okay, I'll do it," Jen agreed. She walked over to the pink telephone by her bed and picked it up. Checking the class list, she dialed Jason's number.

After a very brief conversation with Mrs. Anthony, she hung up.

"His mother says he can't come to the phone," she told Nora. "He can't talk. Can you believe that? He could listen, couldn't he?" Jen was getting red in the face she was so angry with Jason. "Here we are, trying to do everything in our power to help him, and he won't even come to the phone!"

"*Jen.* Remember he's got laryngitis. He's sick."

"Well, what am I supposed to do about that!?" Jen asked, furious.

"Chicken soup — I told you," Nora said.

The next afternoon, Jen and Nora walked into the kitchen at Jen's house, lugging armloads of grocery bags. Each had sacrificed weeks of allowance to finance their marketing trip for the ingredients for chicken soup.

The cost of the fresh vegetables, not to mention a chicken, reinforced their conviction that canned soups and convenience foods in general must be full of poisons and preservatives to be so inexpensive. Not at all what a sick person needed for healing. Jason would have their own homemade special chicken soup.

"Made with care," Jen said. "That's the main ingredient!"

Just then, Jeff appeared in the doorway. "And what, may I ask, is going on here? You girls sign up to make dinner for the Russian army?" He eyed the bulging bags.

Nora explained what they were up to.

Jen was sure Jeff was hiding a smile as he left them alone in the kitchen.

Within a few minutes, Jen had a gigantic pot on the stove, and Nora was washing the chicken parts. They worked for hours, cleaning vegetables, adding seasoning, cutting up chicken pieces.

Finally, proud of their accomplishment, Jen put a lid on the pot, and the girls went to her room to play Monopoly — and to think about doing their homework.

Jen left the door to her room open so they would be able to smell the wonderful aroma of homemade chicken soup as soon as possible.

Jen got Boardwalk and Park Place. Nora got all the railroads and the Orange monopoly, plus she landed on Free Parking and had big bucks to spend on houses and hotels. By six-thirty, Jen was bankrupt and there were still no deliciously tempting smells emitting from the kitchen.

Curious, the girls went downstairs. There was the pot, sitting just exactly the way they had left it. The lid was on it, everything was in it. But nothing was happening to it. They'd forgotten to turn the heat on under the pot. In two hours, all they'd managed to do was to waterlog some chicken parts and vegetable bits.

"Oh, no!" Jen wailed. "I don't believe it!"

Jeff opened the kitchen door. "Something wrong?" he asked brightly.

The two girls practically burst into tears. Jeff handed out tissues, and then pried the whole story out of them.

"Ah-ha!" he said. "I know just the solution to this problem. It's an old family recipe I learned at my mother's knee. Come on, I'll show you."

Then, while Jen and Nora watched, Jeff brought out two cans of chicken rice soup, opened then, and emptied them into a pot on the burner with equal parts of water. He added a bay leaf. "It's the bay leaf," he explained. "That makes the whole thing authentic. Otherwise, you just have plain old canned chicken soup. This, on the other hand, is a gourmet treat."

A few minutes later, the girls sampled the hot soup and agreed. It was delicious. They'd put a few servings in a thermal container and deliver it to Jason, right after supper.

When Mrs. Anthony opened the door at Jason's house, she seemed more than a little surprised to see two girls delivering soup to her son. A little reluctantly, she accepted the gift, but told the girls, on no uncertain terms, that Jason was sick and couldn't have visitors. They were back on the sidewalk in a matter of minutes.

"Listen, we've got to do something," Jen said.

"Like forget this whole thing ever happened," Nora told her.

"No way!" Nora saw that invincible determination on Jen's face again. "Even though he's sick, Jason has to know about the tournament so he can plan his *katas* and *wazas*."

"Whosits and whatsits?" Nora asked.

"*Katas* and *wazas*," Jen repeated. "It's like a dance or something, where karate guys do these moves that they've practiced."

"You've been reading up," Nora accused her.

Jen nodded. "See, there isn't any combat in this kind of tournament. It's these dance things. *Katas* are done by one person. *Wazas* are done in pairs so it looks like a fight, but it's not."

"I'm impressed," Nora said.

"Chapter one," Jen confessed. "But we have to know that Jason is working on his *kata*, so we've got to talk to him. I have an idea how we'll do it, too," she said mysteriously.

"You mean like we'll climb up the tree near his window and sneak into his room?" Nora asked. She'd seen somebody do that in a movie once. It had looked like fun.

"No, actually, I was thinking we might try the telephone again." Jen said dryly.

Nora laughed at her own silliness. The two of them went to Nora's house, and Nora tapped in the number and asked for Jason.

A few minutes later, there was a squeak. It sounded vaguely like Jason.

"Is that you, Jason?"

"Yessss," he hissed.

Suddenly, Nora got very cold feet. "Jen wants to talk to you," she told him, handing the phone to a now panic-stricken Jennifer.

"Uh, hi, Jason? How are you doing? Oh, don't answer that, we don't want you to strain your vocal cords. Gee, well Jason, there's something we think you ought to know about." She gulped. "We've entered you in the YMCA's karate tournament and everyone in school is going to be there and I'm sure you'll win and you've just got to have a great *kata* and a terrific *waza* . . ."

Jason interrupted with a weird squeaking sound, punctuated by honks and hisses. It didn't mean much to Jen, but it sure was loud. She stopped talking and held the phone at arm's length.

Even from across the room, Nora could hear Jason's reaction. Though neither of them knew quite what he was saying, the message was coming through loud and clear. Still, Nora had enough medical knowledge to know that those noises could be injurious to Jason. She ran over and grabbed the phone from Jen.

"Now, listen, Jason," she said firmly. "You've got to stop making those sounds. It's terrible for your throat. You should turn your vaporizer to high, and then, I want you to — "

Nora would have gone on. She could have talked for some time about good things to do for laryngitis. She hadn't even gotten to eucalyptus. But there was no point in continuing. Jason had hung up the phone.

Nora and Jen exchanged worried glances.

Chapter 11

On Saturday morning, Steve stood in front of the mirror in his bedroom and assessed his predicament.

"Karate," he said to himself. "That's the answer." He picked up the book he'd borrowed from the library the day before and opened to page one.

Karate Stances it said. A picture showed a man whose feet were about a foot apart, knees flexed, and arms lowered, but slightly bent at the elbow. That was the Horse Stance. Steve tried it.

The picture looked fierce. He looked in the mirror. *He* looked silly.

Steve was convinced that karate must be the key to Jason's charms for Jen and Nora. Maybe *Nora* liked Jason more for it, because she was so enthusiastic about everything that had to do with good health and exercise.

He stepped forward slightly with his

left foot and pivoted to the left. *Smooth* he thought, admiring his reflection.

But then, maybe *Jen* liked Jason for his karate because somebody who needed to attract attention the way Jason did would appeal to her soft-hearted nature.

He raised his left hand so it crossed his chest for protection. He lifted his right hand high in the air and slashed down quickly. He looked at the floor to where his imaginary enemy had fallen in excruciating pain. *Tough*. He was tough.

Quickly, he punched forward with his right hand and then his left. His second opponent bit the dust.

Steve was out of the house in ten minutes, headed for the Y.

Half an hour later, he felt like a new person. He paused on the steps of the Y on his way out. He breathed deeply, filling his lungs with cool, refreshing air. He felt wonderful. He'd met Doc Holloway, who had welcomed him to his beginner classes and, moreover, had told him that, as a student, he was automatically eligible to participate in the Kick-Off Tournament. Steve didn't think he'd be ready for competition in two weeks, but he knew for sure that both Nora and Jen would be there — because of Jason.

He sighed happily and walked home, clutching his brand-new *gi* under his arm.

He was confident that he would soon be trading his white belt for a more formidable color.

Jen and Nora sat in Nora's meticulously organized bedroom. Jen loved that room almost as much as Nora did. Somehow, the flowered wallpaper, the neat dresser that had a skirt on it that matched the bedspread, and the white nightstand made a very cozy room. Over the years, they'd spent hours in that room, talking about things — important things, unimportant things.

"Nora, I think we've got trouble," Jen said as she rubbed vigorously at her fingernails with the polish remover.

"Jason didn't sound exactly thrilled — "

"Do you suppose he wanted to keep his karate a secret?" Jen asked.

"Maybe, but then, why did he do that demonstration in the lunchroom?" Nora asked. But there was no answer. "I've come to a conclusion: I think we'd better go over to the Y and *un*-sign him up, or should that be sign him down, for the tournament."

"No way," Jen said firmly. "That would make us look silly."

"The only other possibility is convincing Jason to compete, and it's hard to convince him of anything when we can't talk with him."

"A fine romance this is!" Jen said in disgust, tossing a cotton ball into the wastebasket and capping the nail polish remover.

"Whoever said it was a romance?" Nora asked.

"Steve did, remember? Jason's supposed to be in love with us."

"That never made much sense to me," Nora said. "And just because Steve told us Jason was in love with us doesn't mean we should have decided his love was worth requiting."

"Requiting?" Jen asked.

"That is, or ought to be, the opposite of 'unrequite' as in 'unrequited love.' I'm not sure, though. I just invented it."

"Probably good practice," Jen remarked. "We're going to have a lot of inventing to do — such as inventing a way to convince Jason to show up at the Kick-Off. Unless — "

Nora waited for Jen to continue. "Unless he's actually sick all the way up until the tournament. How about that?"

"Great idea!" Nora said "Except that laryngitis doesn't last that long. We have to come up with something else. And I think we'd better do it in person. Let's go over to Jason's house and see him, even if we *do* have to climb the tree to sneak in his bedroom window."

Jen was ready. After all, they had to do *something*.

This time, Mrs. Anthony let them in and had them wait in the den. It was wood paneled, with rustic furniture upholstered in an old red fabric. It looked very lived-in. Jason came downstairs immediately. He was dressed and his hair was combed. He looked a little pale but definitely better than he had at school.

"You're better?" Nora asked surprised.

"Lots better," Jason said. "I think it was that delicious homemade soup. Thanks for making it."

Nora and Jen exchanged glances. They almost couldn't help giggling. At least they'd done *something* right.

"Anyway, I'm glad you're here. I've got to talk to you two."

"We feel the same way," Nora told him.

"It's about the karate thing you called me about," he began.

"That's just what we want to talk about," Jen began. "Jason, it's time for you to stand up on your own two feet and learn to demonstrate all of your good qualities to others. This karate tournament will give you a chance to do that. You can't decide not to be in it. This is probably the greatest chance you'll ever have to be the hero of the eighth grade."

"I doubt that," Jason said.

"Since when did you start being humble?" Jen asked.

"Listen, give me a break, girls. What do you want from me, anyway?"

Nora was getting the strong feeling that she wasn't going to like what Jason was about to say. He sort of held a pillow up in front of him, as if he was afraid they'd throw something at him when he told them what was on his mind.

"The fact is, I don't know enough about karate to enter that tournament, much less win it."

"Don't be silly, Jason," Jen interrupted him. "Nobody wins medals and ribbons at karate tournaments without knowing something about it."

"You're probably right, but I wouldn't know. See, I've never been to a karate tournament, let alone *in* one."

"You lied about the tournaments?" Jen asked. Jason nodded. "But with all those lessons you had — "

"Wrong," Jason said. "The fact is, I've never had a karate lesson. I don't know a thing about karate except what I've seen in the movies. Not a thing."

"Stop kidding us," Jen said, with more than a note of desperation in her voice.

"I'm not kidding you," Jason said.

Jen jumped to her feet. "Okay, then, if you don't know anything about karate, how come you were able to make that really complicated karate move we saw you make in the lunchroom the other day?" she demanded.

"I dunno," he said, holding the pillow up in front of him again. "Basically, the screw had come loose on my skateboard — remember? — and the wheel jammed. It kind of threw me into the air. I was really just trying to get my balance. If that looked like karate, well, I was just lucky," Jason said.

"Lucky?" Jen asked stunned.

Nora wasn't stunned. She was furious. She began throwing pillows at Jason faster than he could protect himself.

Jen came to her senses. She couldn't stand to watch Nora throw anything else at Jason, particularly since it was she and her big mouth that had gotten them into this mess in the first place.

"C'mon, Nora," she said, taking her exasperated friend by the arm. "See you, Jason. Sorry about the trouble, but I'm glad you're feeling better. We'll try to straighten this all out soon. But not right now, okay?" Jason nodded weakly.

Jen pulled Nora away from Jason and backed out of the room and out of the house.

"I never felt so miserable in my life," Jen confessed to Nora. "I hate to think what we're putting that poor boy through!"

"Miserable?" Nora asked. "*You* feel miserable? It's Jason who should feel miserable. Really rotten, horrible, awful miserable. That little worm! Can you believe it?"

Nora went on, but Jen really wasn't listening. She'd noticed that she and her best friend were each taking Jason's news a little differently. No matter how angry Nora was now, Jen was sure that she'd see eventually that the two of them had to figure out a way to get Jason out of the mess they'd, after all, gotten him into. She was sure they'd find a way.

Nora's anger had not dissipated by the time Jen had left her at her house. Jen had a date at the mall. She hadn't mentioned it to Nora, but Denise had called her the day before. She'd wanted Jen to meet her at Frank's on Saturday at three o'clock. She was terribly mysterious about it, and Jen was very curious. Since Denise hadn't shown the slightest interest in sports, Jen was sure she was having a problem finding a present for Tony, and wanted Jen's advice. Jen was almost never too busy to do something for Tony Hendrix.

She decided to forget the problem of Jason Anthony for a while and enjoy her trip to the mall.

But Jason Anthony wouldn't go away. The whole situation gnawed at her conscience, and she found that the more she thought about it, the worse she felt. Poor Jason, she found herself thinking. She had to find a way to solve the problem that wouldn't make him look foolish, and wouldn't make her and Nora look even more foolish.

Jen got off the bus and headed for Frank's. It was a quarter to three — plenty of time. She glanced in the windows of the stores she passed.

Then she came to the Briar Patch bookstore. Jen always liked to look in the window of the oldest bookstore in Cedar Groves. There were so many books written about so many things that it amazed her.

Microwave cooking for diabetics, gardening without dirt, dieting without pain (*ha!* she thought), and then, next to that one, she found the answer. It was a book on karate: *Karate and You* was its title. Even from outside the store, Jen could see that it promised the novice fast mastery of the fine points of the sport in a few easy lessons.

That was it! She and Nora would teach Jason karate!

Chapter 12

Happy and excited, Jen tucked the karate book under her arm. On the way to Frank's to learn Denise's secret, she had acquired a secret of her own. She wasn't going to share it with anybody except Nora — and, of course, Jason.

She rounded a corner in the mall and entered Frank's. There she saw Denise holding a set of folding oars under her left arm, while balancing a volleyball in her left hand. A tin of tennis balls was perched on the strings of a tennis racquet, which was clutched in her right hand. On the floor at her feet were a jumble of T-shirts and a pile of ski poles. Six boys Jen recognized from the high school were trying to help Denise straighten things out, but Denise wasn't paying any attention to the boys' efforts. Tears were rolling down her cheeks.

Jen hurried over to find out what was

going on but halted when an obviously agitated Frank arrived on the scene.

He stalked over to Denise and bellowed at her: "Help like you, I don't need! Please *go*! And take your fan club."

Denise let her arms fall to her sides. Racquet, oars, and the tin of tennis balls clattered to the floor. The volleyball bounced away. Numbly, she stepped over the heap of clothing and the ski poles. She took Jen's arm, then wheeled an about-face and they left the store. The second they rounded a corner, Denise's quiet crying became hysterical.

Jen was flustered. "Okay, Denise, it's okay," she said, giving her friend a hug to help calm her. But that just made Denise cry harder.

"Oh, Jen," she wailed. "I just wanted to make a difference to somebody. I just wanted to help somebody who needed me! I just wanted to be like *you*, and I was a total failure at it."

Jen found a crumpled tissue in her pocket and gave it to Denise. She steered her to an out of the way bench on the far side of the mall's little waterfall, hoping the splash of the water would muffle some of Denise's crying. The last thing Denise needed now was a crowd.

Denise's sobs subsided enough to describe

the Frank Fiasco, her tale punctuated by coughs, hiccups, and an occasional wail.

"You were trying to help Frank out so people would know you were a helpful person?" Jen asked.

Denise nodded.

"You thought that would make people forget you're rich?" Jen asked.

Denise nodded again. "But then I kept getting confused. How am I supposed to know the difference between an ice hockey stick and a field hockey stick? Frank asked me to get a fishing knife — I brought him a hunting knife. I mean, who cares? Then this mountain of shoes fell down on me. And then, worst of all, the boys showed up — in droves. At first, Frank liked it, but then he figured out that they weren't buying anything. They were just there to see me in action. It was hopeless! I don't blame him for firing me. To tell you the truth, I was awful!" She wailed again.

"Of course you were," Jen said matter-of-factly.

Denise, who had expected sympathy, sat up straight and stared at Jen. "What do you mean?"

"Denise," Jen said sensibly. "You don't know the first thing about sporting goods. You can't be any use at all to somebody when the subject is sporting goods — unless it's a modeling job. If you're going to do something for someone, make sure it's something you're good at, or at least something you're interested in. You *hate* sports, remember?"

"Well, if I didn't before, I do now!"

"So, find something you're good at and care about. When you do that, you'll do it well, and people will respect you. Want to come to the Save the Whales meeting on Tuesday?"

"No, thanks, Jen. That's something *you're* good at. Not me."

"Okay, well, you'll find the right thing. In the meantime, let's get you home."

"I can't go anyplace now. My eyes are all red and my makeup's smeared. I look a mess!"

"Okay, first stop, ladies' room."

When Jen saw that the coast was clear of the group of high school boys, she and Denise made a dash for the ladies' room. While Jen watched, Denise took out her cosmetic bag and, within minutes, repaired a remarkable amount of damage.

"You're incredible, you know?" Jen said, admiring Denise's skill.

"It's nothing, really. Just practice."

"Well, I wish I could do it, Denise. Whenever I cry, my face turns all red and blotchy, and everybody knows for hours afterward that I've been miserable."

Denise put her makeup case back in her purse, and they left for the bus.

After they'd taken their seats, Denise turned to Jen. "I guess the new me has to be a different me from the new me I thought I was going to be," she said philosophically.

"Something like that," Jen agreed.

Half an hour later, the kitchen door slammed behind Jen as she entered her house. She made a beeline for the Morris cookie jar on the counter, helped herself to a half-dozen chocolate chip cookies, and poured herself a glass of milk. Before she could make a getaway, though, Jeff Crawford appeared.

"Oh, good," he said. "I wanted to see you. I had a call from Doc Holloway down at the Y. He told me he had a visit from you and Nora?"

"Yeah, we went to ask him to let — "

"I know what you did. He told me. He also said he was really excited about meeting this kid you talked about — Jason Anthony? I didn't know Jason was into karate, Jen. He's the skinny one with the red hair and freckles who's always on a skateboard, right?"

"That's the one," Jen said. She was getting a distinctly uncomfortable feeling. Somehow while she knew that she and

Nora and Jason were in trouble over this brainstorm, it hadn't occurred to her that Jeff would be dragged in, too.

"Well, I just told Doc that I knew the kid, but didn't know about his karate."

"Well, none of us did until recently — very recently!" Jen said. "But it's going to be okay," she told Jeff. "He'll be ready for the tournament — "

"Oh, I know that," Jeff assured her. "I told Doc he could trust you."

" — if it kills me, or him." Jen finished the sentence under her breath. She grabbed her plate and glass and escaped to her bedroom.

The first chapter of *You and Karate* showed all the karate stances and the basic moves. It looked pretty easy. There were good photographs and diagrams to show how feet were supposed to be moved. The second chapter was more of the same. Nice pictures. Looked pretty easy. And then, best of all, were a bunch of *katas*, so that Jason would know exactly what he'd have to do. Maybe he wouldn't have all the basics, but he could learn to do what the twenty-five photographs showed. It didn't seem like a big deal on paper.

Jen felt optimistic. If she and Nora could teach Jason how to imitate those photographs, and he could compete in the tournament, Jason would be a hero, and she and

Nora would be off the hook with him, with Doc, and with Jeff — to say nothing of the fun they'd have watching Susan Hillard's face while Jason won the trophy.

Yeah, Jen thought, it's just the right thing to do. She closed the book and put her shoes back on. She had to go see Nora and tell her how they were going to spend the next two weeks.

But Nora wasn't quite as enthusiastic as Jennifer. In fact, Nora wasn't one bit enthusiastic. The minute Jen walked into her room and showed her the copy of *You and Karate*, Nora groaned

"You've got to be kidding!" she cried. "We don't know the first thing about karate. Nobody — not even a genius — could make somebody a black belt in two weeks!"

"You haven't even looked at the book, Nora. How can you give up so easily?" Jen could feel her cheeks reddening in anger.

Nora stared at her friend in exasperation. "Me, give up easily? You think that's the problem? No. The problem isn't me giving up. It's you holding on, Jen, this thing isn't worth it. Jason's not worth it. Doc Holloway isn't worth it. I'm sorry if we get Jeff in trouble with his friend, but we're a lot better off confessing now than making fools of ourselves later!"

"You mean you're not going to help me?" Jen asked.

"I'm going to help you. I'm helping you by telling you to give it up. Now."

"No," Jen said firmly. "*You* can back out. *I'll* teach Jason by myself."

Jen turned on her heel and stalked out of Nora's house, seething with fury. And more determined than ever to have Jason win the tournament.

Chapter 13

It took Jen a full twenty-four hours to get up the courage to call Jason. Since Nora had abandoned her, she was feeling discouraged, but she was still determined. She waited nervously while the phone rang.

"Hi, Jason, it's Jen," she said when he answered. "Listen, I've been doing some research and some thinking." She paused, but he didn't say anything so she went on. "I've been reading this book about karate, and I think if you're willing to do it, I could teach you enough to compete in the tournament in two weeks."

"Are you crazy?" he asked.

That was just about what she had expected he would say, and she had an answer to it, too.

"No, Jason. I am not crazy. I am totally sane. I've been reading about karate and trying some of the stuff myself, and, to tell you the truth, it doesn't look all that hard.

I think you could learn enough in two weeks to look like a serious student — not an idiot. Would you like to try?"

"You *bet* I would!" he said.

That was more like it.

"Come to my house Monday afternoon at four o'clock. We'll work for an hour and a half every other day, plus Saturday *and* Sunday. Okay?"

"Right on!" he said.

Jen hurried home after school on Monday. It had been a rough day. She and Nora had barely spoken to each other. Jen had had to shush Jason four times so he wouldn't tell the whole world their secret. She'd also spent some time comforting Denise, because some of their classmates who had heard about the disaster at Frank's were teasing her unmercifully.

"I've got to give away a fresh package of tissues every day!" Jen groaned to herself, feeling the weight of everybody's problems on her own shoulders.

And then, there was also the problem of Jeff. She had to use their basement for a *dojo* for Jason's lessons, but Jeff couldn't know about it because he didn't know that Jason didn't know the first thing about karate. Dragging four sleeeping bags down to the basement for gym mats would be a sign that *something* was going on.

110

"What's the story here, Jen?" Jeff asked her when he caught her on the stairs with the sleeping bags.

"I'm trying something out for a slumber party," she lied.

"If you're going to have a slumber party, you have to get your father's okay."

"I know," she said. "I'm not sure I want to do it, but I wanted to see if the sleeping bags fit in the basement."

Jeff gave her a strange look, but he didn't ask anymore questions. She sighed with relief and continued her project.

By four o'clock, she had zippered all the bags together and laid them out so they'd cushion the floor. It wasn't ideal, but it was the best she could do. Then, she waited for Jason at her front door, so she could run him downstairs without Jeff even seeing them.

It worked. But it was just about the only thing that worked for Jen that afternoon.

After a half hour of trying to launch Lesson Number One, it dawned on Jen that Jason wasn't the most cooperative student. As soon as he learned that he was going to have to work, and work hard, his enthusiasm for karate shrank, and his enthusiasm for horsing around and making bad jokes grew.

Jen's instructor's outfit was a leotard, tights, and a loose-fitting shirt. Jason insisted on wearing a pair of pajamas over his gym shorts and T-shirt.

"This looks like one of those karate things, doesn't it?" he asked.

Jen looked at her copy of *You and Karate*, with the pictures of fierce-looking karate black belts, wearing *gis*. She glanced at the photograph, then at Jason.

"Frankly, I don't see the comparison," she said. "I'm not sure what makes the difference, though. Maybe it's the cowboys on your pajamas."

Jason just laughed. Jen didn't really care. Soon, he would have to get a *gi*. For now, it didn't matter what he wore, so if he wanted to look silly, it was really up to him. "Now," Jen continued. "Let's get on with Lesson One."

"Karate for defense only!" Jason exclaimed, bowing with exaggerated manners.

"Not funny," Jen said. Jason pretended not to hear. "Says here that the name 'karate' comes from the Japanese words for 'empty hand.' That makes sense when you think about it. See, there's no weapon in your hand."

"Ah, but my hands are deadly weapons, you know," Jason said, and then he began jumping around, slashing his hands aimlessly through the air.

112

"I think we're going to have to rename this sport," Jen said. "I wonder what the Japanese is for 'empty head.'"

"Now, wait a minute!" Jason said defensively. "I'm trying, I really am."

"*Very* trying," Jen said. And she meant it.

"Okay, okay," Jason said.

Jen took her position on the bare floor, off the mat, and paced back and forth like a teacher. She held the book in front of her and read while she walked. "The first thing to learn is how to stand and how to sit."

Jason flopped onto the floor. "Lesson One is a breeze," he declared. "When do I get my black belt?"

Jen ignored the remarks. "You sit, with your legs folded under you, sort of like kneel and then sit down, knees in front, big toes crossed behind you, your hands resting easily on your thighs."

For the first time that afternoon, Jason did what Jen told him to. She sighed contentedly.

"Now, bow," Jen said. "Karate is just full of politeness. You bow all the time. You have to learn to bow in a couple of different positions."

Jason put his right hand in front of his stomach, his left behind his back, and leaned so far forward that he lost his balance and his head thunked on the mat.

Jen grimaced. "Jason, it says here that when you bow sitting down, you look at the floor six inches in front of your knees. When you bow standing up, you never take your eyes off your opponent. You bow deeply enough to show respect. If you looked away or down, you would be giving your opponent the opportunity to attack."

"Okay," Jason said, bowing politely, eyes focused six inches in front of his knees on the floor.

Jen smiled proudly. Jason had learned something.

The lesson continued. Painfully, Jen read from the book and demonstrated for her student, showing him the pictures as well. The book urged mastering the three main stances, Attention Stance, Ready Stance, and Horse Stance, before doing anything else.

Jen could get the feel of the stances and do them pretty well herself, she thought. Jason couldn't.

The lesson picked up a bit when Eric appeared, uninvited. He was going through a period of fascination with *Kung-Fu* movies and was eager to join the class. However, like Jason, he didn't want to begin at the beginning.

"Kiaiiiiiii!" Eric shouted, lunging at Jason. Jason countered by grabbing Eric around the waist and swinging him in circles until Eric turned green. Jen intervened.

"That's not exactly karate technique," Jen told him. "It might pass in a wrestling ring, but I don't teach that sport."

Jason released Eric. Jen chased him out of the basement, threatening to tell Jeff about the time Eric had hidden in the back seat of the car while Jeff was on a date with his girl friend, Debby Kincaid, if Eric told Jeff what she was up to in the basement.

Exhausted, Jen turned to Jason. "I think Lesson Number One is over. Lesson Nummer Two will begin at four o'clock on Wednesday in Mann-*dojo*. *Sayonara*, Jason."

He bowed respectfully, and left.

Jen flopped down on the soft sleeping bags and stared up at the ceiling.

"Am I crazy?" she said out loud.

There was no answer.

Dinner that night wasn't any fun at all. Jen's mind was on Jason, and she was so spacy that her father asked her twice if she were coming down with something. In spite of dire threats, Eric almost said something three times about Jen's karate class, and she had to pretend she wanted to have a slumber party in order to explain the sleeping bags to her father.

"That basement is too damp and drafty for a slumber party, Jen," he said. "You can have a party if you want, but not in the basement. There's plenty of space in your room."

"I guess you're right," was all she could say.

Wednesday was no better than Monday had been. After an hour and a half, Jason had barely managed to learn how to stand and hold his arms prior to a match.

On Friday, Jason spent most of the time trying to pronounce "Kiaiii." That was the sound experts made while they delivered deadly blows. Jason couldn't deliver the blows, or pronounce the sound.

Jen retreated to her room after supper that night, almost ready to admit defeat.

"Can you believe this?" she said out loud. She was as convinced as ever that Jason *could* learn karate. She was as convinced as ever that it was the right thing to try to teach him. She just wished he'd move onto something more important than mispronouncing "kiaiii" in a loud voice.

She tried to call Steve. His mother told Jen he wasn't home. Briefly, she wondered where he was. She'd barely seen him at school all week. He'd seemed terribly preoccupied, but then, she had been, too. She called Denise. Denise was home, but she was in a terrible rush to wash her hair and wouldn't stay on the phone long enough to commiserate. Jen wasn't surprised. Denise didn't particularly like Jason and wasn't going to be awfully sympathetic about Jen's difficulties with him.

Three times, Jen started to dial Nora's number. Three times, she thought better of it.

Jen felt terribly alone. She was trying to do something important, something significant. She was working, really, really hard at it and her friend, her best friend in the whole wide world, had abandoned her. She felt a lump rise in her throat. She was near tears. She wanted to do the right thing. She wanted to help. She wanted to help Jason. She wanted to do right by Jeff. She wanted to show Susan. She wanted to succeed. She wanted Jason to come out of his shell, to learn that he didn't have to be shy —

Shy? she said to herself.

She finally fell asleep, her dreams a churning jumble, none of them comforting.

Jen woke up with a start. The phone next to her bed was ringing.

"H'lo," she said sleepily.

"Jen, it's Nora. I was being silly and selfish, and even if good old Jason can't learn a thing about karate in the next week or even in the next decade, I agree with you that we still have to try, whether it's because of Susan or Jeff or Jason, but I know one thing and that is that you can't do it yourself because if I'm not there, you won't have anybody to laugh with later. And besides, you have exactly one week to do the impossible. You can't do it without me. I'm sorry. I un-quit!"

Jen smiled broadly. Was she still dreaming? She pinched herself. It hurt. "Really?" she shouted.

"Really," Nora said. "What do you want me to do?"

"Can you go to Frank's and buy a *gi* for Jason?" she asked. "Class starts at one-thirty today."

"I'll be there," Nora promised, and Jen knew she would.

Jason was as excited as a little kid when Nora gave him the bag with his *gi*. He pulled the outfit out of its wrapping and held it up for display. It was a pair of plain cotton drawstring pants and a matching jacket with a heavy tie belt. White. Jason disappeared into the bathroom to change his clothes. Jen and Nora waited quietly for the New Jason.

Then, the bathroom door opened. There was Jason, but in a way, he didn't look like Jason any more. He walked out, stalking proudly. In spite of the fact that the *gi* was just a few pieces of cotton sewn together, rumpled cotton at that, and not really very different from pajamas (without cowboys), the *gi* seemed to transform Jason. Suddenly, he looked like a karate master.

"Look at that," Nora said. "One hundred and five pounds of I'm not sure what!" She and Jen exchanged grins.

"Let's get to work, Jason. Today we begin your *kata*."

"Hai," he answered, having mastered the Japanese for "yes," and then he bowed respectfully.

Jen began explaining what he was going to have to do. "Okay, here's a list of the things you'll use in your *kata* to show your skills at the black belt level: Bow, horse stance, crossed arm block, outward arm block, upward slash, cross body parry, forward slash, guard block, fisted crossed arm block. . . ."

"You're kidding me!" Jason interrupted, wilting visibly.

"No, I'm not. Pay attention."

"But I can't do all that stuff!" he wailed.

"We know you can't," Nora said. Since she'd changed her own mind about the project, she certainly wasn't going to let Jason back out. "That's why we're here: So you can learn. Now you've got the outfit, so I'm sure you can do these things."

"Right," Jen said, sounding as encouraging as she could. "And we've even got pictures, see?" She held up the book.

"Yeah, I see," he said. But he sounded glum. "I'm pretty sure I can't learn all that stuff by next Saturday. To tell you the truth, I thought all I would have to do to learn karate was to punch people and kick them. I didn't realize I'd actually have to work."

Jen took one step toward Jason and put her hands on her hips. "Nobody's punching you, Jason. Or kicking you. *Yet*." The final word was so threatening that Jason snapped to attention and bowed politely.

Chapter 14

On Sunday afternoon, Steve Crowley was listening intently to Doc. Karate lessons had required his total dedication and attention, both while listening to the instructions and executing them. Every cell of his brain was focused on doing what Doc said.

"Karate is a spiritual, as well as a physical, activity," Doc told the class. "When you learn to focus your entire being on one task, you will learn about your own spirit. Understand?"

"*Hai, Sensei,*" the class answered in unison.

"Now it may seem that the things you learn first in karate are pretty simple. But believe me, anything you ever do that requires as much focus as karate is not simple and is important. At the Kick-Off next Saturday, for example, I would rather see you perform one perfect block than an entire *kata* with twenty imperfect blocks. Understand?"

"*Hai, Sensei,*" the class answered.

"Okay, now we will study blocking techniques."

Steve loved every minute of it.

At Jen's, another karate class was taking place.

"Says here that karate's spiritual," Jen said, looking up from the book.

"Wwwoooooooooooooooooh!" Jason wailed.

"Not like ghosts and spirits," Nora said, planting her hands on her hips. "Spiritual, like meditation and poetry, understand?"

"I guess so," Jason said. "But I kind of liked the ghost thing."

"You like anything that doesn't have to do with learning karate," Nora accused him.

"Now that you mention it," Jason began.

"Don't even think it," Nora cut him off in her most bossy, take-charge voice.

"Really, I've got to be honest with you. I love the *gi*, you know, but the rest of it just isn't right for me."

"Don't be silly," Jen said.

"I'm not being silly," Jason snapped uncharacteristically. Normally, he was a sort of happy-go-lucky boy who went along with whatever was happening, as long as he could goof off in his own way. The problem with karate, it seemed, was that he couldn't both go along with it *and* goof off.

"Jason," Jen said, "Nora and I have devoted *hours* to you and to your karate. We know you're not an expert, and even though we sort of got you into this by signing you up for the tournament, you're the one who told *us* you were a champion. If you'd never said anything, none of us would be in this mess. But you did, so it's *your* job to get us out of the mess. Now *focus!*" she shouted at him.

Meekly, Jason dropped to a kneeling position. He bowed. Then he sat back, rested his hands lightly on his thighs, and began to meditate. At least he looked as if he were meditating.

"What are you thinking about?" Jen asked him.

"Lunch," he answered.

Things didn't get any better in school on Monday, either.

"Well, good morning, Jennifer," Susan greeted her sweetly at her locker. "How are things with your red-headed black belt?"

Jen ignored her.

Nora appeared by her side and began taking books out of her locker. "Counting Susan, four people have asked me this morning how Jason is," Jen told Nora. "Everybody's assuming we're going out."

"Just because we spent most of the weekend with him doesn't mean we're going out, does it?" Nora asked.

"I hope not," Jen said. "Things are weird enough without that. Anyway, the day I thought I might be interested in Jason Anthony, I was suffering from a rare tropical disease."

"What's that?" Nora asked, her medical interest piqued.

"Insanity," Jen told her, and then slammed her locker closed.

"Did you hear their new album?" Mia Stevens asked as she joined them on their way to their first class.

"Whose?" Jen said.

"Insanity," Mia told her. "They are the *most*!"

Jen and Nora burst into laughter, leaving Mia confused.

By Monday afternoon, Jason's karate skills were only slightly improved since his very first lesson. After Jason's attempt to quit and the girls' violent reaction, he'd resigned himself to at least one more week of lessons. He tried his best to pay attention and learn something from his devoted teachers. It wasn't easy.

By Thursday, he had learned what most of the moves were in the *kata*, but he wasn't very good at them. One or two of the blocks actually looked passable to Jen and Nora's untrained eyes. Although he could muddle through the moves while Jen shouted instructions from the sidelines, it seemed impossible that he would remember the sequence for the tournament.

"Jason, you've got to get this *memorized*," Jen shouted at him.

"I've got a rotten memory!" he shouted back.

Jason focused. More or less.

On Friday, they did a final run-through of the *kata*. Actually, they did about eight runs through it, and none of them was any better than the one before it. In fact, it seemed that each time Jason did it, it got worse. On the eighth run-through, Jason kicked with his left foot (when he was supposed to be kicking with his right foot) and completely lost his balance. He landed sitting up with an unceremonious thunk on the sleeping bags that cushioned the basement floor. For a second, he stared blankly ahead. Then he lowered his upper body to the floor and closed his eyes.

Nora dashed to his side. She took his right arm and felt for a pulse. She lifted his eyelid.

"Get me water," she said to Jen.

"Boiling water?" Jen asked.

"No, cold water. He's not going to have a baby. He just passed out."

Nora checked his pulse (okay) and respiration (normal) while Jen brought a bucket full of cold water.

"Do I get to do it, or do you?" Jen asked.

"Be my guest," Nora said. "It's the best medicine in the world."

With that, Jen lifted the bucket high and tilted it. A long tongue of cold water spilled over the rim of the bucket and headed straight for Jason. As the first wave struck its target, Jason sat bolt upright. Then, he raised his hands to protect himself from the rest, but he was too late. Jen had directed the water to land on top of his head. And it did. Jason was soaking wet.

Nora offered him a hand. He took it and stood up. "I guess it's real important to remember to kick my right leg there, not my left, huh?" Jason asked. "I sure won't forget that again real soon, but I'm going home now. I'll see you tomorrow at the Y at nine-thirty, okay?"

The girls watched silently as he dripped his way out of Jen's basement.

They took apart the *dojo* that Jen had constructed so carefully with the sleeping bags and put the wet sleeping bags in the dryer.

Jen slammed the dryer door and triumphantly pushed the "start" button. "Now, let's go to the mall and do something for ourselves," she suggested.

"Way to go!" Nora agreed.

Chapter 15

"Now, just what *does* the well-dressed Karate teacher — sorry, I meant the well-dressed *sensei* — wear to a tournament?" Jen asked Nora. They were standing outside of the earring boutique at the mall.

"Egg on her face," Nora said.

"Or crow?" Jen suggested.

"No, I think you eat that."

"Do you think Jason might have a chance?" Jen asked. Nora could feel the nervousness in Jen's question.

"Sure he has a chance," she said. "If — and I'll admit it's a pretty big 'if' — there's a sudden outbreak of typhoid fever in town so that nobody who's ever studied so much as one minute of karate can come to the tournament — including the judges. Under those circumstances, Jason would have an outside chance!"

Jen stared at Nora for a second, and then burst into laughter. It felt very good. "You know, I've been pretending for so long that there was a possibility of his doing this right that I almost forgot it's absolutely out of the question."

"The real question then, is, What *will* happen tomorrow?"

"No, the real question is, Which one of us in going to buy those earrings that say something in Japanese." Jen pointed to a pair of mother-of-pearl earrings with a silver inlaid Japanese character.

"I wonder what it means," Nora said.

"Let's go try them on," Jen said, taking Nora by the arm and leading her into the boutique.

Steve stepped out of Frank's Sporting Goods, which was across the walkway from where Jen and Nora were giggling conspiratorially. He had come out to the mall to get himself a special *gi* that he'd seen advertised for sale at Frank's. He held his package securely in his right hand. He was eager to get back home and try it on for the Tournament the next day.

But he paused to watch Jen take Nora's arm and drag her into the store. He wondered what they were going to buy. He wondered what they were laughing about.

Jen and Nora always had the best times together, he thought, and he really liked being with them. The three of them could laugh so hard at dumb things they all enjoyed. They were a great trio.

Something about the word struck him. *Trio.* That meant three people. Three of a kind. That's what he and Jen and Nora were. What could he have been thinking of? he asked himself. They were both neat girls, but he wasn't in love with either of them — or if he had been, he wasn't anymore. What he really wanted was to be their friend, their good friend.

Was the romance over before it had really begun? Yes. It was.

With new resolve, Steve followed Jen and Nora into the earring store. He'd missed them. Being in love obviously wasn't all it was cracked up to be. Being friends was terrific.

"Say, Jen, Nora!" The girls waved to Steve through the glass door of the store and invited him in.

"Come help us choose some new earrings," Jen said.

"What she really means is come convince me *not* to buy these gigantic ones with the shells on them."

Steve glanced at the pair of earrings in Nora's hand. "They'll look silly on you. Don't buy them! You'll hate them tomorrow."

"That bad, huh?"

Steve and Jen nodded in unison.

"Now, if you want something interesting," he suggested, "Why don't you try these?" He held up a pair of panda earrings.

"Yuck!" Nora said.

"Just trying to be helpful," he said.

"If you really want to be helpful, you'll come with us to Temptations and have an ice-cream soda."

Fifteen minutes later, they all piled into a booth at the back of Temptations and ordered ice-cream sodas. Jen and Nora chatted about the earrings they hadn't bought and Steve thought about the sudden switch in his feelings. It was okay, he decided. Things were back to normal now, and he liked them that way. Romance could be exciting, but he didn't want his relationship with Jen and Nora to be exciting. He wanted it to be open. Honest.

"Say, what did you get at Frank's?" Jen asked.

Steve had almost forgotten. "Oh, nothing much," he said evasively. He wasn't ready to be *too* honest. "Just some stuff."

Jen and Nora didn't really care what he'd bought at Frank's. They were just pleased that whatever it was that had caused him to act so strangely was apparently over with.

"Say, Stevo," Nora said. "I've got to ask

you something." Steve shifted nervously in his seat. He had a feeling he knew what was coming. Nora noticed his discomfort, but she asked anyway. She had to know. "Why did you tell us Jason was in love with one of us?"

"I *did*?" he said, surprised. That wasn't what he was expecting her to say, at all.

"Yeah, at Lucy's party," Jen reminded him. "You told us that Jason was in love with one of us, but he didn't know which one. Jason's hardly shown the slightest romantic interest in either of us, since then. So, where did you get that idea?"

Steve could hardly believe what he was hearing. How could Jen and Nora have confused his declaration of love? Actually, when he thought about it, it didn't make any difference how the message had gotten mixed up. It was probably good luck: It got him off the hook! "Gosh, I don't know," he said. "Maybe I just got confused."

"I guess you did," Jen said. "But it's all right with me. I don't want Jason in love with me. Things are tough enough having him as a friend!"

Before Steve had a chance to ask Jen what she meant by that, Jen saw Denise walking past the shop. Jen tapped on the window until she had Denise's attention and then waved to her to join them.

Denise, Jen was pleased to see, had a big

grin on her face. She nodded happily and then disappeared around the corner to reach the door. A few seconds later, she appeared at their table. Steve slid over on the seat, making room for her.

"You look like the cat that swallowed a canary!" Jen said to Denise.

"And I feel like it, too," Denise told them. "It's the greatest thing, Jen. You were absolutely, totally right."

"I was?"

"Oh, yes. You told me I was crazy to try to do something I didn't know anything about. So, I spent some time figuring out what I *am* good at. It wasn't so hard to come up with the answer. I'm good at fashion. Dixon's had an ad in the paper for their Teen Fashion Panel, and I called them right up. I just got out of my interview. Congratulate me, I'm on the panel!"

"That's fabulous, Denise!" Jen cried, leaning across the Formica table to give her a hug. "What do you do?"

"Well, the Teen Panel meets once a month to discuss new fashion ideas and to make recommendations to the store's buyers. In addition, we get to preview the new clothes each season *and*, once a year we each get to accompany the buyer on a trip to New York! Can you believe it?"

"If you help choose what they sell, we'll all be dressed better," Nora said. No matter how she may have felt about Denise as a friend, she knew Denise had better fashion sense than anybody else at the school.

"You mean that, Nora?"

"I really do, Denise. That's a great thing for you to do. It'll help us all."

"It will?"

"Yes, it will," Jen assured her.

They talked on about Denise's new project and how fantastic it was. Jen was particularly pleased because she had told Denise to do something she was good at. For the first time, Jen realized that she might have used a touch of her own advice. After all, karate wasn't exactly up her alley.

Oh, well, she sighed, scooping up ice cream from the bottom of the tall glass. Tomorrow was another day. She shivered at the thought.

Chapter 16

Saturday morning. Jen woke up with the first streak of light — if she'd been asleep at all. She wasn't sure of that. As well as she could remember, she had been turning from her left side to her right, over onto her back, onto her stomach, all night long. She was worried. She was worried about whether Jason would make a total fool out of her and of Nora and of himself, embarrassing Jeff, and annoying Doc while he was at it. Jason could actually do all of those things — and then some — not to mention providing grist for Susan's mill. Jen just hoped he'd come through.

Jen had been worried about the tournament long before she'd turned out her light. She'd been worried when she'd spoken to Nora at nine last night. But Nora didn't have any words of comfort. She was worried, too.

"Look, Jen. We've done the best we could

with a rotten situation. We've tried our absolute hardest, right?"

"Right," Jen had agreed.

"So, if Jason makes a fool of himself, he makes a fool of himself. That's all there is to it," Nora had said matter-of-factly.

"No, it's not. If he makes a fool of himself, he makes fools of us, too. And then, he won't have any more confidence than he did — in fact, he'll probably have *less* than he started out with, and we'll all be worse off, don't you see?"

"Well, there's nothing more we can do about it, now."

"Sure there is," Jen had said. "I'm going to make him a list of the moves he's supposed to do in his *kata*, and when he gets to the Y in the morning, I'm going to write them on the palm of his hand."

"How's that going to give him confidence?" Nora had challenged.

"It's not, but it may possibly give *me* confidence!"

"Go for it!" Nora had told her, laughing.

Jen spent the rest of the evening abbreviating the list so it would fit on Jason's hand. It was too abbreviated. No way would Jason understand "Hs-st; x-arm blk; otwd-a-b; upwd /." She wasn't even sure he knew what cross-arm blocks or upward slashes were!

Finally, she threw her pen and paper across the floor and turned out her light.

"No wonder I didn't sleep," she said out loud in the morning.

When Jen and Nora got to the Y, Jen was astonished to see the number of kids from the eighth grade class who had come. Most of the competitors had a parent or two in the audience. Some had a brother or sister, too. Jason had a large cheering section. It was awful. Jen's promotional work had really paid off.

"Oh, no. We'll never live this down!" she groaned to Nora, mentally attempting to blend into the woodwork.

"Actually, I've got it figured out," Nora whispered to her. "The humiliation is going to be so tremendous that nobody who likes us is going to think we had anything to do with this. It's all going to fall on Jason's shoulders!" Nora said brightly.

Poor Jason, Jen thought. Then something else occurred to her. There was no sign of Jason.

Both girls scanned the crowd over and over again, but there was no Jason. For the first time, it occurred to Jen that Jason might totally chicken out. And while that had some appeal, it was the worst possible outcome. At least if he tried and failed, that was something. But not trying at all? Jen shuddered at the thought.

When the gong announced the beginning of the tournament, they still hadn't seen Jason.

"I don't believe this," Jen said to Nora.

"I'm afraid I do," Nora told her.

"It never occurred to me that he'd totally fink. Did it occur to you?"

"Yes, I'd thought of it," Nora said.

"Why didn't you tell me?" Jen asked.

"Because you had enough awful things cluttering your brain. You didn't need that, too."

Jen looked at the program. The tournament was divided into four parts: beginner, purple belt, brown belt, and black belt. Each part, except the beginners, would have *katas* and *wazas*. Jen had a modest sense of security knowing that at least she'd read the book right. And now she more or less understood what skills the tournament was judging.

Until Jason showed up, there was nothing for Jen and Nora to do but watch. They found seats for themselves in the arena and listened to Doc explain the very complicated point system he'd devised. Since there wasn't any combat, it wasn't as if the one who was alive at the end of the match was the winner. There were so many points for attempting complicated moves, so many for succeeding, so many for perfect execution, and so on. The highest possible score was 100.

Jen leaned over and whispered in Nora's ear. "If I understand what he's saying, Jason's guaranteed three points — the one's he'll get for spelling his name right in the register."

"*If* he signs in," Nora said ominously.

Jen felt a knot in her stomach. She stared glumly into space.

"Jen!" Nora tugged at her sleeve, bringing her back to earth. "Look!"

Jen looked. There, in the center of the arena standing next to Doc, was Steve. In a *gi*.

"I didn't know Steve was one of Doc's students," Nora said.

"He must have just started," Jen reasoned.

Nora put her finger to her lips to shush Jen, who was about to say something else about Steve. Doc was announcing the people in the white belt demonstration for beginners. One by one, the students began performing their *katas*. Steve would be last. Jen and Nora watched, fascinated.

"So *that's* what it's supposed to look like!" Nora said.

"You and I never saw anything like that

from Jason, that's for sure," Jen agreed. "It's really quite beautiful, you know — almost like a dance."

Jen nodded.

Then it was Steve's turn for his *kata*.

He came out onto the mat and bowed respectfully to Doc. Then he bowed to the audience. He looked so solemn. Jen shivered.

Steve's *kata* was brief. The whole thing didn't take more than thirty seconds. But he'd managed to do three different kinds of punches and had demonstrated four blocking techniques. It was wonderful. As Steve finished and bowed, the eighth-graders who'd come to gawk at Jason began clapping and shouting and yelling for Steve. From where they sat, Jen and Nora could tell that Steve was embarrassed about the attention he was getting. Even Doc was clapping.

Doc came out into the arena and shook Steve's hand. When everybody had stopped clapping, Doc told the audience that Steve had only been studying karate for two weeks. That started the eighth-graders yelling again. Jen and Nora were yelling with them, proud as could be.

With all the excitement about Steve's fantastic performance, Jen and Nora had almost forgotten the reason they were there. Until they saw Jason.

Just as the crowd was sitting down and Doc announced the contestants in the purple belt category, Jason rolled in. Literally. He was moving very carefully, cautiously balanced on his skateboard. Jen and Nora knew something was strange about the way he was moving. But they had to look twice to see what it was. He was pushing himself on the skateboard with crutches. His left leg was totally encased in plaster.

"Oh, no," Jen said.

"Oh, yes," Nora said.

Chapter 17

"You're not going to believe this," Jason began, as he eased himself into the seat next to Jen.

"You're right about that," Jen said before he could go on.

"Well, I just got back from the emergency room," he continued.

Nora stood up and hovered over him. "And you're going to go right back to it," she said threateningly, menacing him with a downward slash — a karate technique she figured she'd learned better than he had.

"See, I was practicing last night and this morning," he said.

"I'm glad to know you practiced at all," Jen said icily.

"And then — "

"Go away," Nora said abruptly.

Jason knew when he wasn't welcome. He

stood up and rested his left leg on his skateboard. He sort of rowed himself on the skateboard with his crutches to an empty seat at the rear of the audience.

"I don't believe his nerve," Jen said.

"I don't believe his broken leg," Nora said.

"Shhh!" said the person behind them.

During the next hour, Jen and Nora almost forgot their troubles. They were really fascinated by the demonstrations. It all seemed to have very little to do with the clumsy, inept flailings they'd seen from their alleged black belt, Jason Anthony. In fact, what they watched in the arena had so little to do with Jason that they very nearly forgot all about him.

When the final trophy had been awarded, the crowd began to split up. Jen and Nora watched as the seventh- and eighth-graders left the gym, talking loudly among themselves. At first, Nora and Jen were afraid *they* were being discussed, or that Jason's bizarre entrance with skateboard and cast would bring them more grief. But, then, Jen and Nora listened to what was being said. The Cedar Groves Junior High students weren't talking about Jason. They were still talking about Steve.

"Wasn't that *something*?" Camille Esposito, a seventh-grader, said to her friend.

"I never knew he was such an . . . uh. . . ."
She struggled for a word. "Athlete," she
sighed.

Jen and Nora stifled their giggles at
Camille's tone of voice. She was obviously
developing a crush on Steve.

"Nora," Jen said as they slid out of their
seats and moved toward the door, keeping
a low profile just in case anybody wanted
to say something to them about Jason. "I
think we may be off the hook."

"Jen, I don't think I've ever been more
relieved about anything since the day I figured out how to fix the blender in shop
class."

"I remember that day. This one's better."

"I think we deserve a celebration. Let's
go to Temptations, and I'll have a blue-
berry yogurt sundae, and you have my
permission to have something highly non-
nutritional, if you want it," Nora said.

"You mean something high in calories,
saturated fats, cholesterol, and refined
sugars?"

"It's your circulatory system," Nora declared agreeably. They linked arms and
headed for the door.

Just as they reached the steps of the Y,
Steve Crowley joined them, grinning
proudly.

"Hey, Steve, you were fantastic. And

what a secret you were keeping from us! Just what were you doing at the mall yesterday, buying yourself a *gi*?"

Steve nodded sheepishly.

"Well, you were great," Nora told him. "And with all that screaming from the kids who came to laugh at Jason, you're the eighth-grade hero."

"Yeah, the last person who applied for that job wasn't qualified," Jen muttered, remembering their once high hopes for Jason.

"Thanks, girls," Steve said. Together they walked to Temptations.

The three of them found a booth near the door of the shop and slid in around the table. As Jen glanced around, it seemed to her that nearly everyone who had been at the tournament had now come to bulk up on sweets. Everybody waved to Steve and called out congratulations. It was the picture Jen had been imagining when she'd first gotten the idea of a friend succeeding in the karate competition. It just turned out to be a different friend. A better one, too.

"So, when did you start your karate lessons?" Nora asked Steve as soon as they'd ordered.

"About two weeks ago. When you two got so interested in the subject, I thought maybe there was something I might like about it, too. I never actually thought I'd like it as much as I do, though."

"It really *is* fun, isn't it?" Jen asked, understanding for the first time that it could be fun — as long as she wasn't trying to cram six years of study into the unwilling head of a total karate klutz.

"Yeah, it is," Steve agreed.

"Oooooooooh! Steve!" It was Camille Esposito — the seventh-grader who'd been almost speechless trying to describe Steve on the way out of the tournament.

Steve turned to watch her as she brushed through the crowd and slid into the bench next to him. Of course, he'd known her for a long time. She'd always been in the class below his. But he'd never really noticed her before. Suddenly, he saw her as if for the first time. Her curly black hair circled her round face, accenting her big brown eyes. When she blinked, her eyes sparkled. When she smiled, as she was doing now, she had the loveliest dimples. He hoped she'd smile a lot.

A wave broke under his heart.

Camille cooed sweetly at Steve. Jen and Nora exchanged glances and stifled grins. Camille was being more than a little obvious. Steve didn't seem to mind, though. For a few minutes, Camille occupied his complete attention, telling him how cool he'd been and how strong he was and what wonderful coordination he had.

"Well, you know, I didn't exactly, you know — uh, I only just. I mean, I'm not really good, uh, like if I'd been — well, a long time, uh, sort of student. You know?" he said to Camille, blushing and getting an other-world look on his face.

"There's something familiar about that look," Nora whispered to Jen, suddenly recognizing the sort of tuned-out, mixed-up Steve they'd seen around school and at Lucy's party only two weeks ago.

"And that sound. Looks like he's going vague and silly on us again," Jen said.

"No, actually, I think he's going vague and silly on Camille, if you know what I mean," Nora observed.

"You mean this weird behavior is a symptom of love?" Jen asked. "But if that's the case, why was he acting so strangely with *us*?"

"Beats me," Nora shrugged. "But it's clear as a bell, he's got a crush on Camille."

"Ding," Jen agreed.

Nora surveyed the mob scene in Temptations. Her eyes rested on Susan Hillard, who was standing about ten feet away. She was watching Steve with such concentration that she didn't even see Nora watching her.

"Look Jen," Nora said, nudging her. "Eighth grade viper."

"I wonder what she wants. Why doesn't she come over and gloat about Jason?"

Nora watched Susan carefully. There was a look in Susan's eyes which told all. "She's not thinking of Jason. Unless my eyes deceive me, Susan's got a crush on Steve."

"The same Susan who originally got us into this mess with that snide remark about the boys at our school?"

"Yes, that same Susan."

Camille finished telling Steve how wonderful he'd been at the tournament and slid back out of the booth. "See you," she said, waving good-bye from a foot-and-a-half away.

"Yeah," was all Steve could muster in return.

Just then, their order arrived. For a few minutes, they were all occupied with figuring out how to attack their treats.

Then they heard a newly familiar thump-whirr, announcing Jason's approach along the sidewalk outside Temptations.

"Oh, no," Jen said.

"What's the matter?" Steve asked.

"Jason," Nora explained.

"You hear what happened to him this morning?" Steve asked.

"Whatever it is, I don't believe it," Nora said.

"Believe it," Steve told her. "I was there." The girls sat forward in their seats, and listened curiously. "Well, he got to the Y really early. He told Doc he was going to practice. He was working on some moves, and I was watching him because I was practicing, too. At first, he looked really awful and clumsy. I couldn't believe he was actually going to be in the tournament."

"Tell me about it," Jen said in disgust.

"I am telling you about it," Steve said. "Then Jason got on his skateboard and started doing blocks. They weren't very good, either. Then, the skateboard hit a waxy spot on the floor or something and started shooting out from under him. He bolted up into the air and executed a fantastic edge-of-foot blow, followed by a high stamping kick. Then he did three arm blocks in quick succession, and a right-left hammer blow. That was real black belt stuff, you know. It was beautiful, until he landed. That was a disaster. I think I heard the bone snap."

Nora winced. "You mean that cast is for *real*?" Nora asked.

"You bet it is. Funny thing about it, though, is that somebody with as much skill as Jason should have landed so badly.

Even Doc was surprised that somebody at Jason's level should have had that trouble."

"Personally, I'm surprised, too," Jen said.

"About the landing?"

"No, about the take-off. Jason always does his best moves when he's falling off his skateboard!" Jen and Nora caught each other's eyes, and the next thing they knew, they were laughing too hard to explain. The very best news of all, though, was that Doc had seen him fall off his skateboard and thought he was good, too. Jen and Nora were completely, totally, off the hook.

Steve waited for more of an explanation, but when none came, he shrugged. "Well, I'll be interested to see him next year in the Kick-Off."

"Me, too," Nora agreed.

"Coming through! Coming through!" It was Jason pushing his way through the crowd, still using his crutches to propel himself. He arrived at Jen and Nora's table and sat next to Steve without waiting for an invitation.

"Listen, girls, I'm really sorry about this morning. I know you were disappointed, but — "

"That's okay, Jason," Nora said. "Steve explained what happened. I'm sorry if we gave you the impression that we didn't believe you. I hope your leg doesn't hurt too much now, does it?"

"Oh, it's not bad," he said, trying to sound brave. It wasn't very convincing. "The important things to me are that you understand what happened to me and that you believe me. I'd really feel terrible if you thought I'd let you down."

"It's okay, Jason," Jen assured him.

"It is?" he said. When she nodded, he stood up again quickly and rolled over to the counter to order himself a banana split.

"You know, he's really awfully good on that skateboard," Jen said thoughtfully. "I wonder if he's ever thought about doing it seriously — you know, like competitively."

Suddenly she had an image of Jason scooting along the sidewalks, hot-dogging through the halls, and hopping up the stairs on his skateboard. She remembered the outstanding midair reverse he'd done, too. "All he'd need would be just a bit of coaching. We've got a nice smooth floor in our basement — "

"You're kidding!" Nora said in horror.

"We could read up on skateboards, you know — "

"You're *crazy*!" Nora shrieked.

"I'm kidding, I'm kidding," Jen shouted. "From now on, Jason can work on being a hero on his own. He doesn't need our help."

"Promise?" Nora asked.

"Well. . . ."

Nora plucked the carob bits off the top of her sundae and began throwing them at Jen.

"I *promise*!" Jen yelled.

Who is taking very candid photographs of the eighth grade and putting them up all over school — and why? Read Junior High #7, THOSE CRAZY CLASS PICTURES.